PRAISE FOR SARAH MACLEAN

"Sarah MacLean is unparalleled. I will read *anything* she writes."

— EMILY HENRY, #1 NEW YORK TIMES BESTSELLING AUTHOR OF *HAPPY PLACE*

MacLean writes her first ever contemporary story, and demonstrates that whether her dukes are prowling 19th-century Covent Garden or are camera-shy 21st-century lords, they're equally as tantalizing.

— *ENTERTAINMENT WEEKLY*

"Sharp, sexy, action-packed, propulsive escapism at its absolute finest. We are lucky to be living and breathing in the Sarah Maclean era."

— CHRISTINA LAUREN, NEW YORK TIMES BESTSELLING AUTHORS OF *THE UNHONEYMOONERS*

"Sarah MacLean sets the bar for what romance can be."

— ADRIANA HERRERA, *USA TODAY* BESTSELLING AUTHOR OF *ON THE HUSTLE*

“There is no one in the genre who does it quite like Sarah MacLean does: her books are brilliant, modern, and moving.”

— KATE CLAYBORN, BESTSELLING AUTHOR OF *GEORGIE, ALL ALONG*

"I recommend *anything* by Sarah MacLean."

— LISA KLEYPAS, NEW YORK TIMES BESTSELLING AUTHOR

“Sarah MacLean’s books are *fierce*.”

— JULIA QUINN, #1 *NEW YORK TIMES* BESTSELLING AUTHOR OF THE BRIDGERTON SERIES

A DUKE WORTH FALLING FOR

SARAH MACLEAN

72 SHELTON STREET

This is a work of fiction. Names, characters, places, and incidents are products of the author's imagination or are used fictitiously and are not to be construed as real. Any resemblance to actual events, locales, organizations or persons, living or dead, is entirely coincidental.

First published in stand-alone print, September 2023.

First published in the *Naughty Brits* anthology, September 2020.

Cover Design: Letitia Hasser, RBA Designs

Editing: Julia Ganis, JuliaEdits

CONTENTS

A DUKE WORTH FALLING FOR
Sarah MacLean

A DUKE WORTH FALLING FOR

SARAH MACLEAN

1

These sheep were not storybook sheep.

Sure, they came with rolling English hills and a gentle mist, but these sheep were not soft and fluffy and they did not gently bleat. These sheep were muddy and pungent and noisy.

And they were advancing.

Lilah Rose planted her rain boots into the slick mud of the Devon countryside, lifted her Nikon and stared down the lens as the herd approached, an enormous black-eyed, gray beast leading the charge.

There it was, that familiar thrill, the one that came every time she knew the perfect shot was in reach—the thrill that came with the edge of threat, because she had one chance to get it.

"That's it," she said softly, the words barely a breath. Lilah might not have shot fashion for eighteen months, but twelve years as a style and portrait photographer were instantly there, hardwired as she cooed to the massive ewe. "Just like that."

Click.

The whisper of the shutter summoned the beast, which increased its speed. Lilah backed away, her steps sure. How many times had she photographed this exact personality—foreboding, absolutely certain of its power, and completely unaware of its vulnerabilities? Wasn't that what had made her the most coveted celebrity photographer out there?

It didn't matter how impossible the subject, how impenetrable the personality. Lilah Rose could capture truth on film. She'd photographed playboys and presidents, longtime A-listers and hot new stars, athletes and socialites, billionaires and royalty. And she was great at it.

At least she had been.

Lilah swallowed around her frustration, hot and thick in her throat, willing away thoughts of Met Galas and Oscar after-parties and the three-thousand-square-foot Tribeca loft she'd once called home base.

It didn't matter that at this exact moment, two years earlier, she'd been in that very loft, shooting the cover of the *Bonfire* Silver Screen issue—a famously impossible task. It didn't matter that she'd been the first photographer in thirty years to get every one of the actors on the cover to agree to a single shoot, in the same room, at the same time.

It didn't matter that working with Lilah Rose had been enough for them to agree. Not even thirty, and it had been *her* name that had brought ten sets of famously longtime Hollywood rivals together—in New York City no less!—and without a single superstar screeching for an agent.

It didn't matter that she'd had to sell the studio when magazines had blacklisted her and her own agent and manager had stopped answering her calls, and the celebrities and power brokers who routinely invited her to parties and dinners in the hopes she'd decide to take their picture had seemingly lost her number.

Stars . . . they're just like sheep!

None of it mattered anymore.

What mattered was getting a picture of this damn sheep.

"At me, beautiful. Right for me."

The ewe didn't hesitate to follow directions. She was ten yards away.

Click.

"That's right."

Eight yards. Coming fast.

Click, click. Lilah was fast too. Too much closer and she'd lose the shot.

Her heart started to pound. She loved this moment on the knife's point, the moment before she either got the picture or lost it, and would never get it back. She crouched, changing the angle, making the beast larger than life.

Five yards.

Not low enough.

She sat, leaning forward, ignoring the cold wet that immediately soaked the seat of her jeans. She'd done worse to get a shot.

She waited, checking the frame, the way the late-summer grass swayed in the viewfinder. The sheep advanced, herd behind.

Enough time for a final shot.

Don't blink.

"Come and get me, you gorgeous girl," she crooned.

"I wouldn't pass up that offer, Mabel."

The shutter fired even as Lilah gave a little squeak and snapped her head around to find the source of the cool words—a pair of grimy Chameau boots about six feet away. She'd just begun to raise her attention higher than the laces to the man who'd spoken, when the sheep—apparently named Mabel—reached her. Along with Mabel's friends.

And then Lilah couldn't worry so much about the man, because she was headbutted by the enormous ewe, who was, as indicated previously, decidedly *not* a storybook sheep.

Mabel was *strong*.

And Lilah was down for the count.

"Argh!" she shouted, half indignation and half terror, and did the only thing that came to mind—rolled to her side, tucked her knees, protected her camera with one hand and her head with the other. Bleating and baas surrounded her, along with the pounding of hooves and the distinct funk of wet livestock. She took a hoof to the kidney. "Gah!"

"Christ!" the boots said, loud enough to be heard despite their distance. The word was punctuated with a high-pitched whistle and the deep, heavy woof of a dog that Lilah hoped was big enough to run off—a hundred sheep? A thousand? Infinity. Infinity sheep.

Another collection of urgent woofs, and the sheep parted.

Good dog.

Lilah lifted her head just enough to take stock of her surroundings. The herd passed on either side of where she was curled in a muddy ball, apparently having decided that trampling her was not worth the hassle of—

"Are you all right?"

The words were grumbled from above, equal parts concerned and irritated.

"I'm fine!" she reported, checking on all her important bits before returning her attention to the boots and beyond . . . up, up over a pair of dark jeans, worn in the knees and thighs, past the warm, wheat-colored sweater to the man staring down at her.

Lilah's mouth went instantly dry.

Good lord. And she'd thought the sheep was big.

Anyone else wouldn't be in the best position to judge his size, but Lilah Rose had spent a decade photographing small men from low angles. This man didn't need the angle. He was *tall*. Over six feet. She quickly catalogued the rest of him, broad in the chest and shoulders with a long, straight nose and a jaw that was comic book levels of square, dimpled chin and all.

Take his picture.

The thought was wild and absolutely terrible judgment. After all, she was a half-hour's walk from anything approximating civilization and very likely without cell service, and this enormous man was not for picture taking. Definitely not while he glowered down at her.

Wait.

He wasn't glowering down at *her*.

He was glowering down at her camera.

And then the glower became something worse. Those lips she'd catalogued flattened into something like disdain, colder than the muck seeping through her jeans. She knew that look. She'd had her fill of it as her life imploded and everything she'd worked for fell to pieces.

She'd run all the way to the English countryside to escape it.

But there was no outrunning it, only fighting it.

Lilah scrambled to sit up even as his hands—very big and warm, not that she noticed—wrapped around her elbows and hauled her upward.

In another situation, she would have been grateful for the help, considering there was no graceful way to rise from the slippery mud of a sheep pasture, but she was *definitely* not going to thank this disdainful jerk for laying hands—no matter how big and warm, not that she noticed—on her.

Before she could pull herself from his grasp and tell him exactly what he could do with those hands she did not notice, he released her, putting immediate distance between them, his jaw setting into stone.

"I've seen you people go to some lengths, but nearly getting trampled by a herd of sheep is new."

Lilah blinked. "We people?"

His gaze narrowed. "There's no need to play coy. I'm immune to it—cow eyes or no."

What the hell? "*Cow* eyes?"

"Big. Empty."

Who did this guy think he was? "Wow. You know what? You're an asshole." She probably shouldn't have engaged with him at all, but she'd had enough of men who used intimidation as a weapon.

"To your kind? Absolutely."

Ugh, she took back all the complimentary thoughts she'd *almost* had for this guy. He was clearly the *worst.*

"My *kind*? You mean civilized humans who were having a perfectly nice time before being manhandled by jerks?" She paused. "I don't know what your problem is; *you* approached *me.*"

Lilah turned on her heel and walked away, as gracefully as she could, considering she was covered in mud. The white and gray sheepdog danced around her, enormous tongue lolling out of its mouth.

"Atlas," the jerk said, and the dog immediately returned to his side. He called after her. "Of course I approached you! You were about to get trampled!"

"I would have happily taken my chances, considering what the alternative turned out to be," she tossed over her shoulder before looking to the dog, happily watching her, tail waving wildly. "You did great though, Atlas. You should find yourself a better owner."

"I'm a fine owner. The kind who came to help when you were *lying on the ground*."

"I was trying to get a shot!"

And dammit, she hadn't even gotten it. Or, if she had, it would be pure luck. Which meant she hadn't gotten the shot.

Instead, she'd gotten kicked in the ribs by attack sheep and yelled at by the handsomest man she'd seen in a long time.

Not that she'd noticed.

"So you admit it," he shouted back.

She turned to face him as he strode toward her, his steps sure and firm, as though he'd never dream of slipping in the mud. As though the mud would never dream of misbehaving for him.

In a decade as a style photographer, she'd come up against egos of epic proportions, but nothing like this. This man—he wasn't ego. He was certainty.

There'd been a time when Lilah had been certainty too.

Never let them see you sweat.

She squared her shoulders, and looked him dead in the eye. "Admit what?"

"You're a photographer."

"Why wouldn't I admit it?" She lifted her chin. "I'm the best photographer you'll ever meet."

If she believed this was a man who had ever in his life been surprised, she might have imagined she saw surprise in his whiskey-colored eyes before he caught himself and said, coolly, "If I'm lucky, you'll also be the last one I ever meet. You're trespassing."

Lilah didn't hesitate. "No, I'm not."

"You're on Weston lands. Uninvited."

"How do you know I'm uninvited?"

He raised a brow at her. "Because I'd know if you'd been invited."

Lilah had seen the mammoth estate house on the drive into the property owned by the Duke of Weston—it was hard not to see it. Maybe big old estates came with handsome security details.

Not handsome.

"Castle guard, are you?"

"Something like that."

"You're missing your armor."

"It's being repaired."

"Broadsword?"

"Shall I fetch it?"

She resisted the urge to smile. This was not a man for smiling at. Back to the task at hand—putting him in his place. "Well, apparently you're not the king's favorite anymore, Lancelot. Because I've got keys to the castle."

The cottage on the eastern edge of the estate wasn't exactly the castle, but it didn't matter.

"Impossible," he said.

"Why don't you call his lordship and check?" she said, reaching into the back pocket of her jeans. "I'll lend you my phone."

"It's His Grace, actually."

Lilah, who had photographed six royal families and knew proper forms of address in every one of their countries, smiled. "I don't care."

Something flashed in his eyes, recognition. "Lottie."

Lady Charlotte Arden was a friend of an old art school friend of Lilah's—and had kindly offered up the cottage on her family's estate for two weeks.

Lilah nodded. "Lottie."

"You're at the cottage?"

She nodded, though the descriptor amused her. This "cottage" wasn't a one-room affair. It came with a sun room, a formal dining room, gorgeous woodwork, creaking floors, a big, four-poster bed, a bathtub bigger than her kitchen in New York City, and an ancient, beautiful Aga stove that made a girl wish she had a reason to roast something. "It's very nice."

He grunted. It should have been off-putting. "She should have told me."

"Oh yes, you seem like the exact right person to bring guests a welcome basket."

"I saved you from Mabel, didn't I?"

"Practically rolled out the red carpet."

"I might not have if Lottie had told me you were a photographer." He said the word like someone would say plague. Or cockroach.

"Gosh, it's almost hard to imagine why she didn't."

Truthfully, Lilah would have liked to have had a little warning about this . . . farmer? Watchman? Whatever he was, he was comfortable enough with the owners to call the daughter of a duke by her nickname.

No one had warned Lilah though. She'd received directions to the cottage, instructions to find a key under a rock near the door, and an assurance that she was more than welcome.

Lottie is over the moon to have you at Salterton Abbey! She's a HUGE fan!! Sophie had emailed a month ago, her excessive use of caps and exclamation points throwing the truth of the words into question. *Don't think too hard about it!! It's solitary and YOU'LL LOVE IT, and it comes with sheep, which I assume you ADORE now!!*

Lilah had picked up the email from a cliffside hotspot in Sicily, where she'd been photographing goats. After the hard sell, Sophie had added what she'd really been thinking.

Take two weeks to steel yourself for your return.

Return. Period.

Sophie had left out all the bits that came after return.

Return, after eighteen months out of the public eye.

Return, after her career had been destroyed.

Return, but not to the world she'd lived in for a decade. To a different world. One that might not accept her.

She pushed the thoughts aside and eyed the man in front of her, who, when he wasn't looking so irritated, was probably the poster boy for the Devonshire Farming Society with his broad shoulders and long legs and sure steps and his sweater that matched the barley in the fields beyond and also his eyes—not that she noticed.

She smiled her photographer smile. The one she used to settle starlets and Sicilian goats, princes and Peruvian llamas. The one that had not worked on grumpy sheep, but would hopefully disarm this incredibly grumpy man. "I'm Lilah."

Another grunt.

Her brows shot up. "Your turn, Lancelot."

She expected the irritation that flashed across his handsome face, but she didn't expect the rest of the emotions—there and gone so fast that if she wasn't used to watching the world at shutter speed, she wouldn't have noticed. Suspicion. Surprise. And something she might have discovered was longing if she'd been able to study the film.

He ran a hand through his hair and a lesser woman would have called it endearing. "I'm . . . " A pause, like he'd forgotten. Like he'd never known.

Lilah waited. A trick of the trade.

Don't blink.

"I'm Max."

And like that, Lilah knew there was a story in this man. This wasn't a family-friendly story though. It didn't come with once upon a time and happily ever after. Because just as his sheep were not storybook sheep, this man was not a storybook man.

Lilah knew that without question. She recognized it, because her life was not a storybook either.

Not anymore.

2

Rupert Maximillian Arden, Fourteenth Duke of Weston and Earl Salterton, was waylaid from entering the Fox and Falcon, one mile from his estate house, by the sound of his mobile.

Pulling the phone from his pocket, Max cast an irritated look at the screen, where his sister's face smiled up at him. He turned away from the pub and lifted the rectangle to his ear, crossing the street into the manicured greensward that marked the center of the town named eons earlier for his family. "I've been trying to reach you for two days."

"Roo!" His sister shouted over the riot of noise wherever she was—no doubt one of London's poshest clubs or some party thrown by some toff looking for a few pictures in *Tatler*.

Max gritted his teeth at the diminutive he'd only ever heard from two women in his life—Lottie, who'd given it to him when she was a baby, and his ex-wife, who'd thought it charming and claimed it as hers when they were at St. Andrews and he'd been too young to stop it.

"Dearest darling Roo!"

His sister always spoke in superlatives and exclamations when she knew she was in trouble. Which was often. The tabloids adored Lady Lottie, activist and street artist by day and delightful scandal by night, and Lady Lottie loved being adored. She was the opposite of Max, who would happily walk into the sea to avoid questions about his status as Britain's Most Eligible Bachelor.

Of course, the tabloids had not chronicled the downfall of his sister's marriage minute by minute.

"I've been *so* busy! I installed a half dozen pieces around Shoreditch a few nights ago, and between avoiding HMP and the rest of it, time has been absolutely impossible."

"It's almost as though vandalism doesn't pay." The words were dry as sand, and held no ring of truth. Max was as wild about Lottie's art as the rest of the known universe.

"I'm ignoring that!" his sister singsonged. "The very moment I was able, I called! Tell me everything! Leave nothing out!" The sound muffled for a moment as Lottie spoke to someone else, then cleared when she returned, deep bass throbbing on her end of the line. "I am fully and completely yours."

Max ignored the obvious untruth, looking round to be sure he was alone. "Your friend is here."

"Right! Lilah!"

Lilah. It was a pretty name—he'd liked it the moment she'd said it in the field. Old-fashioned and perfectly suited for someone with a riot of curls and a riot of freckles.

"You should have told me."

"That she was using the cottage? Why would you care? Is the drafty manor house too much for you? Finally unnerved by the ancestors in the paintings?"

"I care very much that she is a photographer."

"Did she try to take your picture?" His sister was

suddenly very focused, ice sliding into her tone. She might be an absolute loss when it came to remembering—or caring—that her decisions impacted others, but she was fiercely loyal when it came to protecting her family.

"No."

The chill was instantly gone from his sister's voice. "Of course she didn't! Everyone knows she doesn't do celebrities anymore."

The words turned his stomach. "I didn't know she *did* celebrities in the first place."

"Ugh. Roo. It would do you well to read the news now and then."

"Celebrity photographers are not *the news*."

The line muffled again—he'd lost her to another conversation. He sighed and looked up at the sky, clear and sparkling with stars. It was later than he'd thought.

"Sorry! Sorry! I'm back!"

"I'm not a celebrity, Lottie. That's the point."

"We know," Lottie replied, disdain and boredom in her tone. "You're a perfectly ordinary duke in hiding, as though that's a thing. Look. It doesn't matter. She doesn't do portraits any longer. She's photographing wheat or fish or cocoa farms or something for some sustainability thing now. She's far more likely to be interested in the sheep than in you."

I was trying to get a shot!

Lilah had been telling him the truth. A hint of guilt flared, and Max pushed it away. He'd been right to be cautious, dammit.

" . . . all I know is that she needed some time alone, away from the world."

The tail end of Lottie's words collected his attention

again. "Why?" The question was out before he could stop it, and he closed his eyes, instantly full of regret.

Lottie was silent, the heavy throb of music the only indication that she was still on the line.

"Never mind," he said.

"Rupert Maximillian Arden," his sister said at the exact same moment, "are you asking me . . . about a woman?"

"No." His denial was instant. "I'm asking you about the photographer you allowed onto my estate."

"First, it's the *family's* estate. And second, I promise you that Lilah Rose is far, *far* too skilled an artist to care one bit about you."

Lilah Rose. Max resisted the instinct to repeat the full name—softer and prettier as a matched set.

Not that Lottie would have heard, as she was still talking. "—she's certainly not there to take the first picture of the Dusty Duke in a century or however long it's been."

Nine years. It had been nine years.

Max grimaced at the odious nickname that the tabloids had bestowed upon him when he'd turned his back on London and the aristocracy and returned to Devon to take up the work of land steward on the Weston estate. He was about to take Lottie to task for using it with him when she added, "In fact, I'd bet now that she knows you're a duke, she's going to steer well clear of you—with what they say happened . . . "

His admonition evaporated. "What do they say?"

"Sounds like you're asking me about a woman, Roo."

"I'm not. But if she's going to guillotine me—"

Lottie's laugh tinkled through the phone. "Dukes really have it rough these days, don't they?"

He gave a little huff of laughter at the words. "Terrible. Can't even get our sisters to return our calls."

"She's not going to guillotine you. And she's not going to take your picture either." Lottie's exasperation was palpable. "She's not after the title."

She doesn't know I have a title.

That thread of guilt again—but different now. Lingering, as though he should have told her who he was when they were in the pasture, covered in mud and grouching at each other. At first he'd thought she was playing coy and already knew, but then . . . then there'd been something freeing about her *not* knowing. And now—

"What happened to her?" He hated that he asked. It wasn't his business.

And it didn't matter anyway, because his sister answered in her smuggest tone, "She's really adorable, isn't she?"

A memory flashed, Lilah curled on her side in a muddy field, his heart pounding—terrified she'd be trampled. "I wouldn't say that."

"Are you sure?"

Lilah, toe to toe with him in that same pasture, covered in muck, and still ready for battle. Enormous brown eyes framed by thick lashes. Freckled face flushed with frustration and indignation, a smear of mud on her pink cheek.

Wide, full lips that made a man think wicked thoughts.

There was nothing adorable about that woman. She was stunning.

"I'm sure."

"Then you won't mind steering clear of her for two weeks."

"Two weeks!"

"Sorry! Can't hear you!" his sister shouted. "Mobile service is pants here!"

"You're in London."

"Headed into a tunnel! Ring you later!"

"Dammit, Lottie!"

"Bye-ee!"

The line went quiet, the sudden absence of Lottie's cacophonous world making the silence of the greensward unsettling. Max pulled the mobile away from his ear with a choice word. Sisters.

He didn't know how he'd expected the conversation to go—it wasn't as though Lottie ever admitted wrongdoing. She had spent most of her adult life as a tabloid darling because of it. And even if she had offered up an apology for installing a complete stranger at Salterton Abbey without telling him, it wouldn't have changed anything.

Lilah would still be there. For two weeks.

Pocketing the phone, Max crossed the street back to the pub—one of the few places in the world where he was not Weston, Britain's Most Eligible Bachelor, the Dusty Duke, or Roo.

He'd spend the evening the way he spent any ordinary Thursday evening—he'd have a pint, throw some darts, let the ancient old men inside take the piss for a bit. And then he'd go back to the real world, filled with scandalous sisters and an estate in constant need of attention, and a title that came first. Always.

Tonight, he would put all that out of his mind, along with Lilah Rose, whom he only had to avoid for two weeks. Not so hard, that. It was an enormous estate, and the odds of coming into contact with one freckled photographer were slim to none.

He pulled open the door, an unexpected chorus of masculine cheering within. Max's brow furrowed as he scanned the interior of the pub, all leather and mahogany, shadowy corners and—usually—quiet.

John, Richard and Paul—the three older men who were

as much fixtures in the space as the ancient casks in the corner—were turned from their usual spots, rheumy-eyed attention riveted to the dartboard at the far end of the room.

Not the dartboard.

The woman walking toward it, where three red darts were sunk into its bright red center.

Lilah Rose.

He had no reason to recognize her. Her back was to him, and her muddy jeans had been traded for black leggings and a long, white cable-knit sweater that fell to mid-thigh, hiding the curve he'd pointedly *not* noticed when he'd helped her out of the mud. Her hair was no longer piled high atop her head in a messy knot—it was long and wild, the color of roasted chestnuts, gleaming in the gold light of the stained glass wall sconces.

Of course he recognized her.

Even if he hadn't, his body—instantly tight and aware—would have.

"A tenner says ye can't do it again!"

"I'll take your money all night," came her laughing reply as she yanked the darts from the board and turned back to the room.

She stilled, seeing him immediately. He read the surprise in her eyes as her pink lips parted, just barely, on an inhale. She wasn't expecting him either.

She regained her composure quickly, spreading her hands wide, the darts held tight against the palm of her right hand. "No camera."

He should have been gentleman enough not to look her up and down as she stood for inspection. But he wasn't. He looked, cataloguing the line of her long neck, the swell of her full breasts, the flare of her generous hips beneath the sweater, down over the leggings to the red canvas trainers she wore.

When his gaze returned to hers, her head was cocked to one side as if to say, *Finished?*

He didn't want to be.

He cleared his throat. "I was a prat."

She smiled, and he enjoyed the way it filled him up and made him want to earn it. "That's one of my favorite British insults."

His brows rose. "There are others you'd have liked to have used?"

She neared and Max went hot, though whether it was from embarrassment—the boys were watching the scene roll out before them—or from her own frank appraisal, he didn't know.

"Numpty?"

He nodded. "That's a good one."

"Wally?"

Simon—the owner of the pub, who'd been Max's friend since birth—snorted from his place.

Max winced. "Also appropriate."

"Can I say knob in polite company?"

"No one ever called us polite!" chortled John, the rest of the assembled men adding their laughter as Max slid the ruddy-cheeked farmer a look.

"No one's ever called 'im a knob round here either," Richard pointed out.

Lilah looked to Max again. "You're usually better behaved?"

He dipped his head in sheepish reply and said, "I am, actually."

She nodded, her gaze on his, as though she was searching for the truth in the words. As though she expected them to be a lie. She must have seen something she liked, because she finally smiled, wide and winning, stealing some of the air in the room before she said, "So, Max, do you play darts?"

And like that, Max remembered that Lilah didn't know the truth—that he was Duke of Weston. That the castle on the hill belonged to him, and the ten thousand acres of farmlands that surrounded it. That the town, complete with the land the pub stood on, bore his name.

Even here, at the Fox and Falcon, Max hadn't been free of that name. The locals within might have known him since he was in nappies, and they might not treat him with ducal reverence, but they'd never quite treated him as an equal either. He'd been baptized Earl Salterton and spent his years at school with people who befriended him to be close to the title, one of the oldest in Britain. But it wasn't the earldom anyone wanted. It was the other title—the one he'd inherited before he'd had a chance to discover who he was without it.

And along with it, the responsibility for this land and this community and his family—wild Lottie, and Jeremy, his younger brother who had left the UK the moment he'd been able to, bound for particle physics at MIT, where he'd received his PhD and control over a research lab before marrying an equally brilliant virologist and raising two terrifyingly intelligent nephews.

The last time Max had FaceTimed with the family, his brother had leaned into the frame to say one thing—*Met any nice girls?*

It was as tactful as Jez got. He wanted nothing to do with the family business and certainly didn't want it for his boys, who would inherit it if Max didn't meet a nice girl and do his duty. Wife. Heirs. Legacy.

But Lilah didn't know any of that.

She didn't know that he was rich, or powerful, or that half the tabloids in the country would allow her to name her price for a photograph of him. Lottie's words echoed.

She doesn't care one bit about the Dusty Duke.

She didn't know who he was, and it was glorious, because when she smiled, she smiled at *him*, and not at the duke.

And he didn't want that to change.

Not tonight, at least. Not when he could take this rare chance to live out a fantasy he barely allowed himself to contemplate.

Not when tonight he could just be Max.

"I do play darts, in fact."

"Well enough to lay money on it?" Her smile went crooked and he was struck by the fact that his sister was right—Lilah was adorable.

He was right too; she was stunning. And he didn't care that she looked perfectly happy to fleece him out of whatever he had in his pocket.

Max was happy to be fleeced, and Simon and the boys—not one of them younger than seventy—were thrilled to watch it happen. A chorus of chortles rose as he reached for the darts in her hand, his fingertips grazing her soft skin.

Did he imagine that small surprised breath?

He didn't imagine the reaction he had to touching her. Tight, wanting. Just as he'd been in the field. Wanting to do more than compete with her.

Wanting to pull her close and kiss her, steal that breath for himself. Own the pleasure in it.

"Go ahead," she said, softly, and for a moment he thought he'd spoken his desire aloud and she was on board.

But no. She meant the darts.

"As I am feeling magnanimous . . . *and flush*," she added over her shoulder at the men watching, who groaned and jeered in unison, "you can go first."

He raised a brow. "No concern about local advantage?"

"Not in the slightest."

He let his first dart fly and landed it in the outer bullseye. "Oh-ho!" Paul said, brandishing his half-empty pint glass. "Well done!"

Lilah cast a critical eye at the dart before turning back. "Would you like a drink?"

Max raised a brow. "Are you trying to get me drunk?"

"Not at all," she said with a grin. "Unless you think it will help me win."

He laughed, the sensation foreign. When was the last time he'd been free enough to laugh? The last time he hadn't worried about his siblings, the estate, the name, the world beyond Salterton Abbey?

What was the harm in giving himself up to it?

What was the harm in pretending to be Max, the land steward, for a little longer?

His gaze dropped to her lips for a heartbeat, soft and perfect, curved in an open, teasing smile. For him.

One night.

No harm in one night.

Tomorrow, he'd be duke again.

3

Two hours and five rounds of darts later, giddy with triumph, Lilah toasted Max with her second pint. "I'll say this for you, Lancelot, you gave it your very best."

He offered her a very good-natured grin—more good-natured than anything Lilah would have been able to drum up—and said, "A man knows when the battle is lost."

She smiled. "Wherever he falls, there shall he be buried?"

He approached, sandy brown hair falling over his brow as he waved his hand toward the scarred oak floor between them and said in perfect seriousness, "Might as well measure out my grave."

Lilah couldn't help her laugh. He was really very cute. Dangerously cute, if she was being honest, with his laughing eyes and his winning smile and the dimple in his left cheek that matched the dimple on his chin . . . and all that before the rest of his assets—tall and broad with beautiful forearms that she'd had no choice but to notice while they were playing darts.

But she'd made a career out of being unaffected around handsome men. Good genes weren't what made this one handsome. He was just so effortlessly charming. Self-deprecating and funny, no trace of the gruff, unsettling farmer who'd grouched at her camera the other day. In his place, this man who was one of the handsomest she'd ever seen—Sexiest Men Alive had very little on him—and somehow, impossibly . . . easy.

The kind of easy that made a girl wonder what it would be like to wake up on Sunday mornings with him and spend the day in lazy idle. To make Sunday dinner with him. To take after-dinner walks with him. To tumble into bed with him and do it all over again on Monday.

Lilah's life had never made easy possible, but two hours of darts and drinks with this man and his motley collection of friends could tempt her into just that.

He was in front of her then, staring down at her, one dark brow cocked in sheepish curiosity, as though he knew what she was thinking.

As though he was daring her to reach out and try easy on for size.

Dangerously cute. Dangerous, full stop.

She tilted her chin up. "You're lucky I am feeling benevolent tonight."

He reached into his back pocket and extracted his wallet. "By my count, it's fifty quid for the losses?"

She shook her head. She didn't know the going rate for an English farmer, but fifty pounds was a lot for anyone. "The reward is the win itself, don't you think?"

"Not if you lord it over me for the rest of your stay."

"Aren't we on the ancestral lands of a duke?" she asked, all tease. "Do you think he'd mind if I took on the lording for a bit?"

The words were barely out of her mouth when the pub went silent. One of the elderly men's pint glasses settled on the bar with a *thunk*.

Max's gaze slid to the sound, and something flashed across his face. Frustration? Irritation? With her? She followed his attention to the men who had been watching their darts, rosy cheeks gone ruddy against pale skin, their eyes now trained on Max.

He didn't look so easy now.

Lilah couldn't tell if she'd said something wrong or if something had happened that she simply hadn't noticed, but the air had definitely shifted. Grown cooler.

So much for flirting with the hot farmer.

Hiding her confusion and her disappointment, Lilah grabbed her messenger bag from the sturdy stool where she'd left it. "It's late," she said. "I should go."

Before she could sling the bag over her shoulder, the oldest of their audience—a tall, white man, all long limbs and sharp joints, who had reminded her of the farmer from any number of British children's films when he'd introduced himself as John—said, "Do *you* think *he'd* mind?"

The words drew her attention, but John wasn't looking at her. He was looking at Max. As were the other men.

Lilah looked too, though she didn't know why. Her brow furrowed as Max cleared his throat and said to John, "I don't think he'd mind, as a matter of fact."

Confused, Lilah tracked the conversation back to the bar, where Paul, portly and quick with a smile, raised a brow in Max's direction. "*You* don't. Think *the duke* would mind."

Those strange emphases again, and Max, that strong, sturdy, unflappable farmer who took her teasing in stride was gone.

Strong became stoic.

Sturdy became stiff.

Unflappable became unbending.

Not so easy anymore.

The stark change could mean only one thing: there was something Lilah didn't know about Max and the Duke of Weston. Bad blood of some kind, maybe? Which didn't really explain how protective he'd been of the duke when he'd thought she was paparazzi.

Maybe the duke was a terrible boss. Lilah had certainly met her fair share of rich and powerful men who were terrible bosses.

Who were terrible, period.

And Max, out in the muddy fields with his good dog, likely with no choice but to take whatever garbage the lord of the manor doled out. She knew what that was like.

She knew the danger of not taking it too.

He looked away from their audience, and she wanted to do something. To say something. To touch him. Anything that would show him he wasn't alone. But he wasn't looking at her either.

"Have you met the duke, Lilah?" The bartender, this time, who'd introduced himself as Simon. He was in his thirties and handsome, and big as a house, with a broad chest and muscled forearms covered in tattoos.

She shook her head and approached the bar, opening her wallet to pay her tab. "No," she said.

"Imagine that," John said.

"Is that so strange?" she asked.

"Strange?" Simon said, looking to Max, who was watching him intently. "A bit, I'll be honest."

She set her near-empty pint glass down on the bar and plucked a leftover dart from where it had been forgotten. "Don't dukes have things to do besides rolling out the red carpet for guests? Balls to dance at? Rolls Royces to drive? Cravats to tie?"

The men assembled laughed. All except Max.

"He doesn't wear a cravat," Max grumbled.

She smiled. "It was a joke."

He didn't seem to think it was funny. "She's Lottie's friend."

Simon's blond brows rose. "And she hasn't met the duke."

"I'm not really her friend," Lilah was quick to correct. "I've never even met *her*. Lady Charlotte and I have a mutual friend."

"All the more reason for her to meet the duke, Max," John said. "Not every day a girl gets a chance to meet a real live title."

Lilah laughed and shook her head. "It's not necessary. I've met plenty of real live other things, and learned not to believe the hype."

"Right. Lottie says you're a posh photographer," Simon said.

Max shot him a look. "What are you doing talking to Lottie?"

The bartender shrugged one shoulder. "I like to keep up with goings-on." He looked to Lilah. "Who's the poshest person you've photographed?"

"Oh, for—" Max said, looking at Lilah. "You don't have to answer that."

"It's okay," she said with a laugh. "I've taken a lot of pictures. Actors, authors, world leaders, athletes."

Simon whistled, impressed. "All right then, who's the biggest tosser you've ever photographed?"

The one who got me blacklisted because I wouldn't sleep with him.

"Simon! Christ!" Max turned to her. "You *really* don't have to answer that."

"I only ask because she's not impressed by the duke," Simon interjected.

Lilah let the dart fly, watching it land in the dead center of the board. The men assembled shared a collection of impressed looks before she turned back toward them. "In my experience, men who are born with money and power are more trouble than they're worth. And considering the castle on the hill, the duke is a great deal of trouble."

"Oh-ho!" John chortled from his seat.

"Brazen, sayin' such a thing on the man's land," Paul chimed in, though it was less criticism and more delight.

"I don't mean to sound ungrateful. He's got a very cool sister and a beautiful estate that I'm more than enjoying—especially the company," she added with a smile. "Let's just say it's not him . . . it's me."

"He's not a bad geezer," John said.

Max looked to him. "He's not, as a matter of fact."

"I believe you," Lilah said.

"Ugly bastard," Simon chimed in from behind the bar with a wicked smile that, combined with the wicked gleam in his blue eyes, probably made knees weak across the county. "Babes scream just to look at him."

"That much is true," Paul confirmed.

"That is patently false," Max said. "He does all right."

"Good thing he's a duke, is all I'm saying," Paul replied.

"It's not the face I'm worried about," John said, tapping the side of his head and looking straight at Max, "it's the faculties." The men assembled—minus Max—nodded their agreement as he added, "Makes brainless decisions."

"That much is true," Paul repeated.

"Not as a matter of course," Max said, defensively.

Maybe she'd misread the dynamic between them. Someone who didn't like his boss wouldn't be so affronted by criticism of him.

"Nah, but when he does, they're big 'uns," Richard said. "Great fun watchin' the fallout!"

Max let out a low grumble at the words, as though he didn't know whether to defend the duke or agree with the men assembled. Lilah chalked it up to some kind of long-standing cultural view of the aristocracy and tried to change the subject.

"Truthfully, I'm not really a meet-the-duke kind of girl." She looked to Max, surprised to find him staring directly at her. She tried for humor. "I'm more of a meet-the-shepherd-in-a-muddy-field kind of girl."

Paul blinked. "The shepherd . . . "

"Max!" John said, as though he'd just learned the fact.

Simon chimed in. "Course it's Max! What else would he be?"

Someone was drunk. And Lilah was certain it wasn't her.

"Lilah was taking photographs of the herd the other day," Max said, approaching, his wallet still in hand. "We met and I was a . . . "

"Prat."

"Numpty."

"Wally."

"Knob."

The descriptors were offered in unison, in myriad tones of sheer delight.

Suddenly, Max wasn't so stiff anymore. His lips quirked in a small, sheepish smile that made her insides do strange things, especially when paired with the gleam in his brown eyes. "Right."

Lilah couldn't help her own smile. "You really take a beating, don't you?"

"Deserved, innit?" He lifted a noncommittal shoulder, one lock of shaggy hair artfully draped over his brow, like he'd just stepped out of a rom-com. *Easy.*

Would he kiss like that? Easy?

She imagined he would, slow and smooth, lingering like he had a lifetime to explore. And when he did explore? His hands on her? His body against her?

Lilah's heart skipped a beat thinking about how easy it would be to slide a hand up his chest and into that soft hair. How easy it would be to fit herself to him and forget that the rest of the world could be so difficult.

She should leave now. Before she tumbled into something that could only end up a bad idea.

She set her empty glass on the bar with a smile for Simon before looking to the rest of the men who had kept her company for the evening. "As much as I adored this evening, gentlemen, I am out far past my bedtime."

She'd reached into the side pocket of her bag to find a few pounds when Max set a hand on her arm, electric heat shooting through her at the touch.

"At least let me pay for the pint." The words were low and soft, like a promise, and it occurred to Lilah that she might have agreed to anything he'd offered in that particular voice, close enough for the words to vibrate around her.

"That, I'll allow," she said, wondering how her own voice had gone so breathy. "Thank you."

He opened his wallet and tossed several twenty-pound notes onto the scarred bar. Simon straightened lazily to collect the money and the glass. "Lilah, you shouldn't walk back alone."

A chorus of elderly masculine agreement followed,

including Richard's excited addition, "Absolutely not. Too dangerous."

"Dangerous?" Lilah laughed. "What, precisely, is dangerous out here in the middle of nowhere?"

"Can't be too careful. There's tales of marauders."

Her brows shot up. "Marauders."

"Tales of 'em, yes."

"Tales from when, 1700?"

"And more recently," Paul said, all expertise. "We had a highwayman in the 1820s. He took one look at the young duchess and thieved her right out from under the duke."

"Max, tell her," Richard said, hefting a pint in their direction.

She looked to Max, who'd shoved his hands in his pockets and grinned. "It's true. She was never seen again. Legend had it she became a highwaywoman and they terrorized the countryside for years."

"Are we afraid that this nineteenth century Bonnie and Clyde might rob me on the walk home?"

He tilted his head, rubbing a hand up around the back of his neck and over his hair, ruffling it in a way that made her insides do those strange things again. "You never know."

Lilah laughed. "I think I'll take my chances."

He leaned down, his lips close to her ear, and the temperature in the pub was instantly warmer. "There are no marauders."

The words were a rumble of pleasure, and Lilah shivered at his nearness, her heart pounding. If she turned her head, he'd be *right there*. His lips would be *right there*. That easy kiss would be *right there.*

"But it is dangerous."

She sucked in a breath and pulled away, using all her willpower to do so. "What's so dangerous?" she asked, softly, even as his lips curved in that slow smile that made her want to do very bad things.

She didn't think anything was more dangerous than what she suddenly wanted very much to do to this man.

"The sheep are still out there, Lilah."

The laugh came, full of surprise and delight. *Easy.*

What if she took easy?

There was no harm in one night.

"All right, Lancelot. Walk me home."

4

Max closed the door on the Fox and Falcon and the censure of the men inside. Exhaling, he looked to Lilah, turned to him in the warm golden glow of the pub's windows, a curious half-smile on her lips.

"They can be a lot."

Her smile widened. "They're perfect. If someone asked me to close my eyes and describe the contents of a pub in the Devon countryside, those men would be it."

He gave a little laugh. "Three men who've been in those exact chairs for as long as I can remember?"

She nodded. "Fixtures."

"They are that," he said, waving a hand in the direction of the dark road that would lead them back to the estate.

She fell into step beside him. "You've really known them your whole life?"

"Feels like more than that," he said.

"So you grew up here."

The question was so casual. Just conversation. One thousands of other people answered without hesitation on any given day. One he could answer without hesitation. And still, he hesitated.

She looked at him, enormous brown eyes clear and patient, like she'd wait forever for him to tell her the truth.

I'm the duke.

She was going to find out eventually. He should say it. Get it out of the way, before he decided he liked more than the curve of this woman's smart mouth.

But he didn't want to. He didn't want to feel the air shift between them. Didn't want to hear her voice slide into a higher octave when she said one of the things people always said when he referenced his title for the first time.

Oh!

A duke!

You are?!

What is that *like?!*

Have you met the Queen?!

And he didn't want the rest either. The sudden sizing up, the reassessment. The knowledge that every opinion she formed of him after the revelation of his title would be clouded by the title itself.

The unavoidable, malicious whisper: *She doesn't see you. She only sees the duke.*

Worse: *She doesn't want you. She only wants the duke.*

And then: *She doesn't love you. She only loves the duke.*

Her brows rose as the silence stretched between them. "Max?"

No harm in one night.

"I was born here."

She nodded and returned her attention to the road, visible in the bright light of the moon. "And you still live here, with people who care about you."

"For people who care about me, they certainly enjoy taking the piss."

She laughed at that, the sound lovely and rich. "I think that's how you *know* they care about you."

"It is, honestly."

Lilah watched him for a moment and then said, "That sounds like you have proof."

In his darkest moments, as his marriage disintegrated before God and tabloids, it had been those men who'd smacked him surely on the back and bought him pints and let him privately grouse to them. And during those moments, Max had been certain they'd remain private. After all, he wasn't ever going to talk about them.

So he would never know what made him respond, "Let's just say that when your marriage falls apart, you could do much worse than those four."

She didn't hesitate, her footsteps sure as they turned off the road and onto the long drive to the main house. If only Max could take the moment in such stride. In the nine years since its demise, he'd never once spoken of his marriage. To anyone. Not even the men down the pub.

Until this freckle-faced, doe-eyed, red-shoed darts shark had appeared.

Silence stretched between them, and it should have been uncomfortable, but it wasn't. She nodded. "I'm happy you had them, then."

No questions. Just honesty.

She sighed and looked up at the stars, clear and bright against the night sky. "You could do worse than them, and you could do worse than here."

The words were kind and light, but there, in the tail end of them, Max heard it. Wistfulness. Sadness. Nostalgia.

Something else. Something he couldn't name but somehow understood, because it was familiar.

Someone had disappointed her too.

She's going to steer well clear of you—with what they say happened. Lottie's words.

He should leave well enough alone. He shouldn't push. Everyone had secrets. God knew he did. And yet, "What about you, Lilah Rose?"

She slid a surprised look at his use of her last name. "Checking up on me?"

"Wanted to make sure you weren't planning to rob the place."

"The oil paintings are safe." She laughed. "I won't have the wall space when I get back to New York." A pause, and then she added, "Come to think of it, I won't have walls when I get back to New York."

Knowing he shouldn't—knowing it wasn't fair play to ask her for secrets when he wasn't sharing his own—he grasped the string and pulled. "Why not?"

She lifted a shoulder in a little shrug that revealed more than she realized. "I sold my studio space eighteen months ago."

"For what, backpacking across Europe?"

"Around the world, actually. This is my last stop. Ten more days."

"What's in ten days?"

For a moment, there was nothing but the sound of her footsteps as they walked, the steady crunch of her worn red Converse trainers on the graveled path. "I return to the real world."

"What does that look like?"

She shook her head and looked at him, and there it was again, the sadness. The uncertainty. Max clenched his fists in his pockets, resisting the impulse to pull her close and wrap his arms around her. To keep whatever demons haunted her at bay. If he wasn't careful, he'd turn into Lancelot. Pledge her his sword.

And everyone knew what happened to Lancelot. He didn't get the girl. In fact, he was her downfall.

She looked to the main house, windows lit in the darkness. "Does it have a folly?"

The question was so unexpected it took him a moment to follow it. "It does."

Lilah smiled. "Two years ago, I shot Henrietta Wolfe, Vivienne Darby and Margot McKennett at a folly at Highley Manor."

Lottie had said Lilah was an artist, but photographing a trio of Shakespearean actors, each well into their eighties, each made a Dame by the Queen, who were collectively considered Britain's greatest treasure . . . Max couldn't help being impressed. "What was that like?"

Her voice filled with wonder. "Unbelievable. I've taken pictures of some amazing things, but those three? They've lived hundreds of lives in their work, and you can see it in every line of their faces . . . " She trailed off for a moment before she said, "The camera—it loved them."

Max could see her pleasure. Hear her breathless excitement. And he knew, without question, that she had loved that day.

She doesn't do celebrities anymore. His sister's words from earlier in the evening.

Why not? "What happened to the pictures?"

Like that, Lilah closed up. He'd said something wrong. "They were never run."

Sadness again. Loss?

Why?

He didn't ask. Maybe because he knew she wouldn't answer. Maybe because he knew that if she did, he wouldn't like what it revealed.

She filled the silence. "Anyway—before that shoot, I didn't know follies were a thing. I mean, who could imagine that people would build entire buildings for no purpose whatsoever?"

"Not for no purpose . . . they served a very clear purpose of showcasing the aristocratic love of excess."

"I never think of the English as being overtly excessive." She paused. "Estate houses aside."

He gave her a little smile. "Oh, never overt. That's the point. The folly here, which right now serves absolutely no purpose whatsoever, *looks* exceedingly useful."

"Useful in the sense of . . . "

He put on his best ducal accent, the one perfected during years of schooling. "How else are we to guard the northern border?"

She laughed and turned toward him, walking backward up the drive, the moonlight gleaming on her mahogany curls. "Back to marauders, are we?"

He watched her, riveted to her pretty, open face. Wanting to do more than watch it. "I thought we agreed that it was sheep."

She slowed, the laugh trailing off as his words echoed the moment in the pub, when he'd leaned in close and whispered in her ear, the scent of her wrapping around him like sun-drenched linen. It had taken every ounce of his self-control to resist pressing his lips to the soft, warm skin of her neck.

Soft, warm skin that tempted him even now, from beneath the collar of her sweater.

"Right," she said, softly, stopping altogether, turning her

body toward him, and he would have given his whole fortune to know what she was thinking.

Enormous brown eyes, hooded. Full lips, parted.

He didn't need a fortune to know what she was thinking.

Lilah Rose wanted him.

And she wanted *him*. Not the Duke of Weston. Not Rupert Arden. Not St. Andrews or the Mayfair townhouse or the massive estate.

She wanted Max.

Christ, she was perfect here in the darkness, the crisp autumn air whispering through the trees, the night sky like a blanket, the universe closing around them.

He pulled his hands from his pockets, slowly, not wanting to ruin it. Not wanting her to think he'd only walked her home for this. To touch her. To kiss her.

It was true, that. He liked her. He hadn't wanted to say goodnight. Not yet.

And he wanted to kiss her.

But a gentleman wouldn't—

And then her fingers were on the bare skin of his forearm, stroking over the hair there, leaving a trail of fire in their wake, down his arm, over the back of his hand, until they laced into his for a heartbeat, just enough to make him wonder what she would do if he tightened his grip on hers and pulled her close.

Just enough to make him wonder how well she'd fit against his chest.

What she would taste like.

How quickly he could make her sigh with pleasure.

"Will you take me there?"

He'd take her wherever she wished.

No. That wasn't what she was asking.

The folly.

"Now?"

She smiled, and her touch slid away. "No. In daylight. But I imagine it's beautiful at night under the stars."

You're beautiful at night under the stars. "I'll take you there."

"Thank you." The words were soft and perfect, and they made Max want to give her everything she could ever want, just so he could hear her say them again. He wanted to lay her down in his bed and pleasure her until she was sighing them into his ear.

He cleared his throat at the thought and waved a hand in the direction of a turnoff from the main drive. "You're up here."

She looked off to where the light from the cottage shone through the trees, then back to him. "Where are you?"

He waved a hand in the direction of the estate house. "Other direction."

Not a lie.

Not the truth, neither.

Lilah looked back up the path toward the cottage, and he heard the breath hitch in her throat, as though she wanted to say something but wasn't quite sure what it was.

He would have waited there all night to hear it.

Finally, she looked back at him, her brown eyes gone black in the darkness. "Tell me something, Max . . . "

Anything she wanted.

" . . . are there sheep between here and there?"

"Could be," he said, his heart pounding, awareness thrumming through him. He wasn't young and he wasn't a fool. He knew what she was asking. "Shall I walk you the rest of the way?"

She led him through the darkness, beneath the ancient trees that had witnessed any number of lovers headed for that particular cottage in the dead of night over the last three hundred years.

When they reached it, Lilah turned to watch him for a moment, and Max couldn't shake the idea that she was searching for something. Truth? Trust?

Whatever it was, she found it, and her fingers were back, sliding over his, threading through them. Her face tilted up to the moonlight. To him.

"Come inside." Not a request. Command. Pure temptation. Easy to follow.

It was his turn to touch her, to reach for her, his fingers stroking down the side of her face, along her jaw and down the column of her neck. She shivered, leaning into the heat of his hand, bringing one of hers up to hold him close.

His grip tightened, and she pressed herself to him—tight enough that he could close the distance between them without trying. Settle his lips on hers and steal her kiss.

He growled deep in his throat, frustration humming through him. "I can't."

"You can, though."

"The pub," he whispered, setting his forehead to hers, closing his eyes. "The drinks."

"Two pints. Three hours. I'm not drunk, Max."

She stepped closer to him, her free hand coming to his chest, warm and firm like a promise. His fingers flexed. He'd never wanted anything the way he wanted her. But he was trying to do the right thing.

"It's sweet you think you'd be taking advantage of me," she said, softly.

"I would," he said, matching her tone, leaning down and inhaling at the place where her neck met her shoulder, breathing her in as her fingers slid into his hair and tightened, holding him there. "I'm *already* taking advantage of you."

I'm taking advantage of the fact that you don't know who I am. That you don't treat me the way every other woman I've ever known has.

His lips brushed the soft skin of her shoulder, warm beneath the collar of her sweater, and she caught her breath.

"Don't stop," she commanded, pressing him closer, and he responded, his tongue circling against that magnificent, smooth skin, just once.

They both groaned at the sensation.

"Or maybe it's you, taking advantage of me," he spoke to her neck, his lips sliding along the column, over her jaw, to her ear.

Lilah's fingers tightened in his hair, tugging, and he lifted his head at the delicious sting, looking to her. She smiled, and it took all of his willpower *not* to give in. Not to take what he wanted. "I would really enjoy taking advantage of you."

And then she leaned up and kissed him, and he knew he shouldn't, but he let her, groaning into the caress, his fingers tightening on her waist, pulling her closer—was he pulling her? Not really. She was coming for him, fingers sliding in his hair, body pressed against his, all soft curves and perfection, and her mouth—pure, lush, beautiful sin.

She sighed into his mouth, and they took advantage of each other, just for a moment.

Just long enough for Max to slide his tongue against hers, just for a taste. Just long enough for him to know what he would miss when he remembered that he shouldn't be kissing her right now. Just to know her sweetness, so later he'd know what he missed when he lay in his own bed in his own house and stroked his cock and imagined her with him.

She tasted like spring.

But he wasn't the only one tasting—Lilah was stretching up to him, her arms wrapping around his neck, her own tongue meeting his. Exploring him as she pressed against him, her warm body fitting against him as she ended the kiss and whispered, "You taste like autumn."

He went instantly hard and pulled her tight to him with a growl, his hands falling to her ass and lifting her against him, her legs wrapping around his hips as he set her back to the closed door of the cottage with a thud that somehow set them both free.

She exhaled on a low, delighted laugh and looked up at him through her lashes—a lethal combination that sent a straight shot of pleasure through him. "So strong," she whispered, her hands stroking over his shoulders and down his arms, testing the muscles that strained there.

"I could hold you here forever," he said, setting his lips to her neck, her jaw, her cheek, and then kissing her again, meeting her tongue as it darted into his mouth and giving it a long suck, until a little cry sounded in her throat, and she rocked her hips against his, her core hot and perfect and too fucking far away, separated from him by layers of clothing.

He groaned as she increased the pressure there, where he wanted her beyond reason, and they kissed again, heavy and intense. She was like flame in his arms, hot and perfect, and sexy as hell, and the kiss went on and on, rioting through him until time disappeared, and place, and him—leaving nothing but Lilah.

"I could be held here, forever," she whispered, breaking the kiss, looking him straight in the eye. "Max . . . " His name came like a siren's call, punctuated by another slow rock against him.

Christ, she felt good. *This* felt good. Better than anything he'd ever experienced, and he gripped her tighter, pressing into her more firmly, one hand sliding into her thick curls, holding her still as he rocked against her, once. Twice.

She sighed. "Please, Max. One night."

One night.

Temptation incarnate. And what if he gave himself up to it? He'd thought it himself, earlier. One night. One night with her, and without the rest of the world. Max met her eyes, dark pools, heavy-lidded with want. He understood that too. He wanted her just as much. More. When was the last time he'd wanted something so much?

No harm in one night.

Except he knew now, even before he'd had her, that he wouldn't be able to stop at one night. He'd need more for what he wanted to do to her. For how he wanted to consume her.

For the look in her eyes, like she had delicious plans herself.

One night would never be enough.

Max lowered her to the ground in a slow slide that had him gritting his teeth from the pleasure of her body against his, of her indulgent, wicked smile, of her decadent sigh, of the throbbing ache of his cock.

And he lied.

"One night."

5

It was a mistake, of course. Lilah knew it even as she pulled Max through the ancient oak door into the entryway of the cottage. She was going to London and then to New York and she absolutely did not need the complication of a hot British farmer, who was way too perfect for a one-night stand.

Or a one-week stand, for that matter.

This was the kind of man who made you want to stay.

But that was a problem for *future* Lilah. Present Lilah didn't have any problems at all.

She toed off her shoes as Max kicked the door closed behind them and reached for her with a growl, one arm sliding around her waist and pulling her to him.

She wrapped her own arms around his neck as he lifted her again, and she let out a little squeal. There was no three-hundred-year-old wall behind her this time, and Lilah wasn't exactly pixie-sized, but he carried her like she weighed nothing, and he wasn't even winded.

She threaded her fingers into his hair and wrapped her legs around his waist. "So much for the gentleman, huh?"

"Turns out I'm the marauder."

Pleasure coursed through her, pooling deep. "What will you do with me?"

One hand slid up her back, large and warm and firm, and he said, low and dark, "I have some ideas."

"Me too," she whispered, leaning down, her lips a hairsbreadth from his. "Should we see if they match?"

He groaned, his fingers sliding into her hair, pulling her down as he took her kiss, hot and lush, licking over her lips in a rough stroke that set her on fire. How was it that this man kissed like this? How was it that he tasted like wheat and smoke and sun and rain? How was it that he made her feel like she might spend the rest of her life searching for another kiss like this one—addictive and perfect?

They lingered there, in the foyer of the cottage, kissing for what felt like minutes or might have been days, and when he broke the caress it was only because they were both gasping for breath.

Lilah opened her eyes, finding his whiskey-colored gaze on her. "Okay?" he asked.

"Perfect."

He grunted his approval and took her lips again, the world tilting beneath them. No, not tilting. He was walking, headed for the stairs behind her.

She broke the delicious kiss and said, "Wait."

He stopped short, like he'd hit a brick wall, and pleasure shot through Lilah.

"I just want you to know," she leaned back and put her hands to his cheeks, staring down at this big, beautiful man who was carrying her through the house like they were in a romance novel, "I don't have someone in every harbor. I haven't had someone in *any* harbor in . . . a while." She closed her eyes. "I'm making a hash of it, but . . . it's important I say it . . . so, yeah. I choose you."

Something relaxed in her when she said it. Something that hadn't been fully relaxed in eighteen months.

He nodded. "Kiss me again, Lilah Rose." And she did, long enough to soften into his arms. And when she did, he broke the caress to whisper, "I choose you too. And I haven't had anyone in any harbor in a while either."

"Okay." She smiled and kissed him again. "Do you want . . . " She trailed off . . . not quite knowing how to finish the question, but feeling like she should be polite. " . . . a tour?"

His laugh was a low rumble as he stepped onto the bottom stair. "No."

She clung to him as he carried her to the first floor of the house. "Something to eat?"

He stilled on the landing and met her eyes. "Mmm."

The sound curled through her, sending heat pooling to the place where he was hard against her. "Mmm," she repeated, soft and almost breathless. Lilah pointed toward the bedroom she'd chosen. "There."

He was already moving.

Inside, he flicked on the lights and set her down beside the big bed, his warm, strong hands coming to cradle her face, his thumbs stroking over her cheekbones until her lips parted from the soft pleasure of the caress and he leaned down to give her what she wanted, a long kiss that made her squirm. When he lifted his lips, he slid them across her cheek and to her ear. "You like that?"

She sighed her answer. "Yes."

"Mmm." That low growl. God, how was it that a mere sound made her wet? And then his hands were stroking over her hips and waist, up to where she was heavy and aching for his touch. "You like this?"

"Yes," she said, frustrated, wanting him to touch her breasts.

"But you want more."

"Yes, fuck. Yes," she said, the fingers of one hand clutching his strong forearm, the others tangled in his hair.

He gave a low laugh.

She turned to him. "Touch me."

"Tell me where."

She did one better, grabbing his hand, moving it. He exhaled, his fingers flexing over the flesh of her full breast, and she gritted her teeth, wanting her clothes gone. Wanting *their* clothes gone.

"It's not enough," he growled.

She shook her head. "I want more."

"I want it all," he said, and the words came like a confession, as though he shouldn't.

She met his eyes, recognizing the understanding flashing in them. Understanding and something else. Something like hunger. One that matched her own. "Take it." After a long moment studying her, Max released her, and Lilah swayed with the loss of his touch.

And then his hands were on the hem of her sweater, clutching the fabric and pulling it over her head, and Lilah had never been more grateful for putting on a decent bra. He exhaled, reaching for her, one fingertip tracing the scalloped edge of the delicate red lace. "Red." He smiled. "Like your shoes."

"I like red," she said, her breath hitching as that wicked finger found the peak of one hard nipple, swirling over the lace, making her want to scream.

"Take it off," he said, the command like a shot in the room.

She didn't hesitate, reaching behind her to unclasp the bra before she looked up at him and said, "You take it off."

His gaze flew to hers and his hand fisted around the fabric, pulling it down, baring her to him. He stilled for a moment, watching. Riveted, and her nipples went impossibly hard under his scrutiny. "Look at you." He lifted a hand to his lips, rubbing his gorgeous mouth as though he was starving and she was a meal. And then his gaze came to hers. "You're beautiful."

She blushed.

"Shall I tell you more?"

Yes. Yes yes.

"You are." He was reaching for her again, that finger returning, circling until she thought she might lose her mind if he didn't— "Does it ache here?"

She looked to him, full of need, and told him the truth. "So much."

"Mmm." That sound again. Pleasure. Hunger. And then he took the tip of her breast into his mouth, working her gently until she sighed and her fingers came to his head, holding him there even as she wanted to beg him to move, to do more.

"God, Max, yes."

Another low growl and he released her. "Do you like that?"

"I can't remember," she replied. "Do it again."

He laughed against her skin as he moved to the other breast, giving it the same attention, long, slick, rhythmic sucks that opened a line of pleasure straight to her core, as though he was already inside her.

And then, like he knew what she wanted, he lifted his

head and stole her lips in an equally delicious kiss, walking her back until her knees hit the bed and she sat, Max lowering himself with her, but not to the bed.

To the floor.

To his knees.

Between hers.

Anticipation flooded her as his hands found the waistband of her leggings and pulled, taking her underwear with them over her hips and thighs, down her legs, until she was completely bare.

Lilah was suddenly very aware of being naked in that room, in the glow of the porcelain bedside lamp, while this man—big and strong and beautiful in his own right—studied her.

And he did study her—his whiskey gaze tracking over her skin, devouring her, making her ache.

Instinctively she moved to cover herself, but Max was having none of that. "No," he rumbled. "I want to look."

Before she could reply, he touched her again, his strong hands stroking up her legs, searching for and finding all the places that made her shiver. Her ankles. The backs of her knees. The soft swell of her belly, the undersides of her breasts.

He kissed her at the base of her neck, his tongue making a little circle until she sucked in a breath and he laughed again, low and sexy as hell.

Those hands disappeared, back to her knees, easing her thighs open. "I want to look," he whispered, the heat of his breath against her skin like a promise. "Will you let me?"

She bit her lip. "Yes."

"Mmm." He sat back on his heels, his hands sliding along the soft skin of her thighs, pressing her open, wide.

And then his eyes were on her, and she couldn't stop

herself from watching him. God, he looked like he was about to devour her. And she wanted it. Badly.

She moved, flexing her hips beneath his gaze, setting off a low rumble in his chest. His hands stroked again, down to her knees and back up over soft skin, until they found the tight curls at her core, brushing over them once, twice, until she rocked against him again. "Max."

"You like that?"

"No," she said. "Stop teasing me."

He parted her folds, gently. "Christ, you're wet. That's for me, isn't it?"

She lifted her hips toward him, the movement rewarded by one of his long fingers stroking, just barely—just enough to make her hiss her frustration at the barely there pleasure. "*Max*," she said again.

The bastard laughed. "That?"

"More."

The word came out harsh and directive, and Max's gaze shot up to hers. "Now *that* . . . that *I* like."

And he gave her what she wanted, that finger stroking over her slit, up and down over her straining, aching flesh, back and forth, never quite getting to where she wanted him most.

She grabbed his wrist. "Now."

The word was barely out of her mouth and he was there, his finger on her tight, aching clit, circling, pressing, stroking, until he found the rhythm that threatened to break her apart.

She rocked against him, and her eyes found his as he worked her, over and over. "Fuck, you're beautiful," he whispered. "I'm going to watch you come again and again, all night long."

Whatever he wanted. She'd give it to him. "Yes."

"But first . . . "

His touch was gone in an instant and Lilah cried out, the sound garbled and frustrated, even as he was pressing her thighs wide and lowering himself between them.

"Shh, love," he whispered. "I know."

"Max . . . " His name came out on a cry.

"I know, love. But you see, I changed my mind," he said to her core, the words soft temptation against her as he tucked his shoulders, wide and perfect, between her thighs, holding her open for him. "It turns out I do want something to eat."

Her laugh immediately became a groan as he set his mouth to her, his tongue tracing the path his finger had blazed earlier along her soft heat, savoring the taste of her as he licked and kissed in long, lingering strokes, as though they did not have one night . . . as though they had forever.

And Lilah, unable to do anything else, gave herself up to the twin pleasures of feeling . . . and watching. Because Max watched her the whole time, his eyes on hers, hot and dark and full of need, reading her pleasure as he manipulated it. As he controlled it.

Her fingers found his hair again, clenching there, holding him to her. "Yes," she whispered as she rolled her hips against his magnificent mouth, in time with his steady, languid licks. "God, *please*."

She watched his eyes light with a wicked gleam as he growled against her and gave her what she wanted, finding her clit, swirling his tongue around it and flicking over it, slow and delicious, until she couldn't watch anymore, her eyes sliding closed as she lay back on the bed and gave herself up to this magnificent man.

One of his hands came to the swell of her stomach, warm and enormous over her, pinning her to the bed as he continued to fuck her with his mouth, flattening his tongue against her and working it against her, again and again.

She fisted his hair and rocked against him. "God, yes, don't stop," she whispered, and he didn't, this gorgeous man, instead pushing one thick finger of his free hand into her, pressing deep, searching, fucking her, and he didn't stop.

He didn't.

He worked her and he played with her and he fucked her with his hands and his mouth and his *eyes*, still watching when she flew apart, coming up off the bed, her own eyes opening, instantly finding him as she came, and came, and came, his name on her lips, laying waste to her thoughts.

And he stayed there as she came down from her pleasure, his fingers stilling, his tongue gentling, stroking in long, slow licks that sent delicious tremors of pleasure through her until she found the strength to release the hold she had on his hair and fall back against the bed, sated and thoroughly pleasured.

No. Not thoroughly. There was another thread of need there.

Need to be closer to him.

Need to be with him.

She sat up and he was there, meeting her kiss as she came for him, consuming her with lips and teeth and tongue so she could taste herself on him. In him. With him. And that taste, that moment, that kiss—

"You are wearing too many clothes," she whispered, reaching for the hem of his sweater, yanking it up over his head and sending it flying across the room, instantly forgotten.

Her eyes went wide as she took him in, broad and muscled with years of working in the fields, the opposite of every man she'd ever been with before. Those men had all been lean and lanky. But Max . . . well.

Name was destiny.

Her hands stroked over his wide shoulders, his broad chest, down the ridged muscles of his abdomen to the waistband of his jeans. She stilled, her eyes on his. "Do you mind if—"

One side of his mouth kicked up in the sexiest smile she'd ever seen. "I do not."

Her fingers were on the fastenings of his jeans then, tearing open the button and lowering the zipper, her curiosity taking over as she reached inside the shadowy opening and found him, hot and heavy and *huge.*

Her eyes went wide. "Max," she said softly, nibbling at his earlobe when he grunted his reply. "Turns out you *do* have a broadsword."

He stilled, a little exhale the only indication that he'd registered the words before he ran his hand through his hair, over the back of his head, and looked away, sheepish. "Sorry."

She couldn't help her laugh. "That's the most English thing I've ever heard."

His gaze shot back to hers. "What?"

"Apologizing for your penis size." She stroked it, measuring its length and girth beneath soft fabric. "Listen to me, Max. You have *nothing* to apologize for."

He growled, low and dark, in reply, and that hand that had been the hallmark of his chagrin reached for her, cupping her chin. When he kissed her, it wasn't apology. It was claiming.

And she *loved* it.

Without breaking the kiss, he removed his clothes. She scooted back onto the bed as he joined her, eager to feel him bare in her hand. She pushed him to his back and came up to straddle his thighs. "Let me see."

The gorgeous man did, putting his hands behind his head and watching her as she explored him, straight and thick and beautiful. She couldn't stop herself from stroking him in a long, slow slide, crown to base. Again. And again, this time marveling as a drop of liquid revealed itself as his foreskin slid back. She rubbed it into his skin with her thumb, and he swore softly.

Her gaze flew to his at the sound. "You are so beautiful," she whispered, leaning down to press a kiss to the sensitive head, to taste him, earthy and salty and perfect, and he cursed, one hand coming to her hair, stroking her curls.

"Lilah," he growled. "Not like this."

She lingered there. "Just a taste, Max. Just one . . . please."

"Christ." His hips rocked into her grip.

"Just once," she promised to the velvet tip of him. "Just once, and then I want you to fuck me." She sucked him down as he groaned her name, loving the feel of his cock, thick and heavy on her tongue, and the sound of his filthy mouth thick and heavy in the room around them. And then he was pulling her up off him and rolling her to the bed, and she was squealing her displeasure. "Not fair!"

"What's not fair is that you are a witch."

She smiled, feeling powerful enough for it to be true, and spread her thighs, cradling him between them, his heavy, hot shaft against her. "Shall we try for real magic?"

"Mmm," he said, stealing another kiss, quick and dirty, before saying, "Don't go anywhere."

He was gone to his wallet just long enough to fetch a foil packet and return, climbing up her body again, placing long, lingering kisses along the way, until she was writhing beneath him, wet and ready.

The broad head of his cock was at her entrance, and Max pressed into her, slowly, aware of his size and clearly wanting to give her time to adjust. Lilah strained for more and he held back, sinking into her by impossible measures, each time pulling out slowly, until only the head of him stayed with her. Until they were both breathing ragged, devastated breaths.

And only when she was wild with need for him did he give her what she begged for. He began to thrust, slow and —yes, so easy—so smooth and even and perfect, like they'd been doing it for a lifetime and not just one night. "Oh, God," she said, her arms around him as she tilted her hips up to his. "Yes."

"There."

"More."

"Please."

"*Max*."

And then he was fucking her, hard and smooth and unleashed, and he was whispering the filthiest things in her ear, rough and beautiful, and she was doing as he asked, sliding her hand between them to rub her hard, straining clit again, and he was lifting himself up, giving her more room, and thrusting deep and fast and she'd been right.

It was so easy. Like home.

It would have scared her if she'd let it, but she didn't have time to think about it, because electric pleasure was coursing through her and she was coming hard around him, harder than she could ever remember coming, milking his own release from him and reveling in the harsh shout of her name on his lips as he came in long, heavy thrusts that sent ripples of pleasure through her.

He was glorious.

It was glorious.

When they'd recovered, Max collapsed onto his back, pulling her over him, pressing a kiss to her temple and tucking her into one of his big, warm arms, as though she belonged there.

And the strangest thing was that she *felt* like she belonged there.

He rumbled again, that rolling "Mmm" pure satisfaction beneath her ear, and the sound sent a little thrill through her even as it settled her, heart pounding, into something else entirely.

Something like happiness.

She'd think about that in the morning.

But first . . . sleep.

6

Lilah woke to sunshine and the smell of coffee, both of which were unexpected, as she was usually up before the sun, and it had been a long time since she'd had someone to make coffee for her. Equally unexpected: waking in sheets that smelled like autumn leaves and sex.

Max.

He'd stayed.

She'd woken twice during the night, the first time to his lips on her skin, pressing warm, soft kisses over her shoulder and neck until she'd rolled to her back and directed his touch to where she wanted him. He'd made her come twice before she slipped back to sleep.

The second time, it had been nearly dawn, the sky outside that perfect charcoal that came just before light. Max had been asleep, and it was Lilah's turn to wake him with lips and hands, to follow his wicked, wonderful instructions until they were both sated.

This time, it was morning, and he could have left.

But he'd stayed.

She should have been unnerved by the realization, but she wasn't. In fact, as she stretched in the beam of warm sunlight and catalogued the lingering effects of the night before—a tight muscle here, a delicious twinge there—she was filled with an undeniable thrill.

Minutes later, having pulled on a pair of soft yoga pants, a tank top and a cardigan, brushed her teeth, and ensured she looked properly, artfully mussed, she made her way down the ancient creaky staircase to the kitchen of the cottage. Hesitating in the doorway, she watched him, tall and broad and freshly washed. Wearing different clothes than the night before.

He hadn't just stayed. He'd left . . . and *returned.*

He stood at the scarred wooden counter next to the stove, chopping something that he had to have found wherever he'd found his new clothes, because last she'd checked, the cottage refrigerator contained a bottle of rosé, a carton of milk, half a wedge of Stilton, three Cornish pasties and an apple—none of which was producing that delicious smell.

"I've heard about these English fairies," she said, moving into the room. "Bringing clean clothes and eggs"—she peeked around him—"and thyme?"

"I had to feed Atlas," he said, setting the knife down and looking to her. "I thought you might be hungry. I kept you up late."

And like that, the air in the room shifted, the memories of the night before between them, full of pleasure. "I am hungry," she said, not meaning for it to come out quite so soft. Quite so wanting.

But it did, and his gaze heated, and she wondered what he'd do if she suggested they table breakfast and head back up for round four.

"Lilah Rose," he said, the words a delicious rumble. "I

have plans for this morning and if you keep looking at me like that, you're going to ruin them."

She inhaled at the words—direct and perfect, like this was normal, every-day-after-ordinary-sex breakfast and not extremely not normal, morning-after-excellent-first-time-sex breakfast—and smiled, coming closer. "Would we say *ruin*?"

He reached for her then, one big hand grabbing the waistband of her tank top, fisting the fabric and pulling her close for a kiss that should have been a normal daytime kiss and was instead extremely not normal and incredibly sexy, his tongue stroking deep, sliding against hers until she sighed and went loose in his arms. Only once she clung to him did he release her. "Pour yourself a coffee and wait for breakfast like a good girl."

Unf.

She did as she was told, telling herself that responding so thoroughly to being called *good girl* was offset by the fact that she was absolutely going to sexually objectify this wildly handsome man while he cooked her breakfast.

Tucking one leg beneath her, she sat down on the wide bench on the far side of the large oak table where she'd set up shop with her laptop and equipment earlier in the week, and watched him work, moving two saucepans around the ancient Aga and navigating the kitchen with ease, finding everything he needed without pause.

"You know this house well," she observed. He did pause then, his shoulders stiffening just barely, just for a moment —so quick that you'd have to be incredibly skilled at reading people to notice.

She waited through the hesitation—a lesson learned in years of training. Hesitations revealed truth. *Don't blink, or you'll miss the shot.*

"I lived here for a bit." Her brows shot up, but she bit her tongue, staring at his broad, hunched shoulders. She was rewarded for her patience when he added, "When my marriage was falling apart. I didn't want to be in London, and I didn't want to be at the main house. So I stayed here."

Lilah looked down at the table then, at the map of the grain, crossed with scars and dings and divots, and her thumb traced the edge of a knot in the oak, imagining him here, nursing a broken heart.

They'd both come here to mend wounds.

They'd both come here to start fresh.

"Well," she said, finally, returning her attention to his back, "I think you should have stayed for the stove, honestly. I'm in love with that stove. If I *were* a thief, that's what I'd take."

"This cooker weighs at least a tonne and was installed before you were born, Ms. Rose; you'd need a team to nick it." He laughed, grabbing two plates from a shelf nearby and turning one perfect omelet and then another onto them before he collected napkins and forks and approached the table.

She took a moment to admire his lean hips where his dark Henley met the waistband of his worn jeans. "Why do you think I'm making friends with a very strong farmhand?"

He set the plate in front of her. "Mushrooms, herbs and goat's cheese. Eggs fresh today from the girls. How's that for farmhand?"

She blinked. "You collected *eggs* this morning?"

He shrugged, taking the chair across the table. "It was on the way."

She wasn't sure it was, but she wasn't about to turn down a home-cooked meal. She lifted a fork and took a bite. "Max, this is *delicious*."

"It's nothing." He dipped his head, that blush spreading across his cheeks again. If Lilah had more time with him, she'd make it her personal goal to summon that blush once a day.

"It's *not* nothing. I should know. I've been living in Airbnbs for eighteen months." She waited for him to look at her. "Thank you."

He didn't look away then. Instead, he replied with absolute honesty, "Thank *you*, Lilah Rose."

And it was Lilah's turn to blush.

He watched her for a long moment, and she could see the pleasure in his gaze. She wanted to preen beneath it until he cleared his throat. "So, you've seen the world."

"Not nearly the whole of it, but a lot more than most."

"And what was that like?"

She looked to her gear at the end of the table. "At first? Terrifying."

He waited patiently.

She took another bite of the omelet, using the time to find her answer. "When I left New York—" She paused, not quite knowing how to tell him the truth without telling him the truth. "Well, I didn't know if I'd ever be able to take pictures again. I sold my studio and packed my gear and left with my passport and a list of old friends from art school who I thought I might be able to beg a couch from here and there."

"And?"

"And about four months in, I was in India and a friend told me a story about a woman who lived nearby, who was changing the world."

"How?"

"Organic fertilizer. Devi drove me to a farm in Andhra Pradesh and introduced me to Aarti Rao, one of the preeminent minds in sustainable farming. She's developed a natural treatment to protect seeds and young plants from fungus that can devastate crops and livelihoods on small farms across India."

"Sounds a long way from the red carpet."

She grinned. "I know a lot about cow urine now."

"Fascinating stuff. Would you like a job here?"

She shook her head. "Too late. Dr. Rao is on the board of Common Harvest, an NGO in support of sustainable farming—"

He nodded. "I know it. Salterton Farms is a member."

"So you know that Common Harvest is always looking for ways to elevate sustainable farming. To make it . . . "

"Cool?" he supplied, his tone indicating that he found it anything but.

Lilah laughed. "Don't be so quick to doubt. People love the idea of sustainability. Farm-to-table is everywhere, farmers markets are having an absolute renaissance, there are Instagram accounts devoted to celebrity farmers all over the world."

Max couldn't hide his surprise. *"Why?"*

She pointed a fork at him. "Do not underestimate the appeal of a beautiful person holding a piglet!"

His brows shot together. "A piglet!"

"Maybe you and Mabel should team up," she suggested, trying to keep a straight face.

He grimaced at the suggestion. "I'm not sure either of our dispositions would suit."

"Fair." She laughed. "But the truth is, the world is getting bigger and bigger, and people are feeling more and more disconnected, and so we are all thinking more about what it means to be closer to the things that keep us . . . " She searched for the word. Found it. "Happy."

"And farms make you happy?"

This one could.

She bit back the reply and pointed to the omelet on her plate. "How much of this came from here?"

"All of it."

"And you too, so farms make me very happy today."

He smiled, small and satisfied, and she resisted the urge to swipe the plates to the floor, crawl across the table and kiss that satisfaction from his lips. He was proud of his work, and that was something she understood.

"So. You're to make farming cool."

He didn't know that not long ago Lilah Rose could have made anything cool—even cow urine.

"That's the job," she said. "Aarti lobbied hard for Common Harvest to hire me, and when I told them what I wanted to do, they agreed. I drove back out to her lab and took pictures of her. And then I traveled the world, taking pictures of a dozen other people in their labs and on their boats and farms and with their beehives."

"And was that terrifying?" he asked.

She shook her head. "No. That was incredible. Exhausting and challenging and weird at times . . . but really incredible."

And it had been. She'd found her feet again, camera in hand, taking portraits of interesting people. Which was what she'd loved doing in the first place.

"Where are the photos now?"

"They'll be shown at the Common Harvest gala in London. Next week."

A pause, and then, "The end of the journey."

All those months traveling, taking pictures, trying so hard to rebuild herself and forge a new path back . . . She nodded. "Nine days. And then back to the world."

And maybe, just maybe, back to her life.

"And will they do it? Make farming cool?"

If he'd asked her that question two years ago, she would have answered, categorically, *yes*. Two years ago, Lilah had been on top of the world, the most in-demand photographer around. She'd been able to choose her clients, name her price, and set her standards. She'd been in the perfect place—old enough to no longer be a wunderkind, young enough to have a lifetime of opportunity ahead of her.

And then, in an instant, the walls of her carefully constructed palace came tumbling down.

Frustration flared, along with self-doubt and disappointment, all emotions that she'd learned never to show. But she wanted to show it here, in this place, with this man who had no tie to the world of wealth, privilege, glamour and high society that had made her famous. He didn't care that she was famous. And there was freedom in that.

Space for honesty.

"I don't know," she said. "But if anyone can make it cool, it's me."

"A lifetime of practice."

"I've made a lot of people cool."

"Would I have seen your pictures?"

She was good at her job, and wasn't ashamed of it. "Probably."

Max watched her for a long moment, long enough that she wondered if she'd said something wrong. "Show me."

Her stomach flipped. "Show you what?"

"Show me what Lilah Rose can do."

She almost didn't. But it had been so long since someone had seen her work and judged her on its merit, and not on the stories they'd heard—the lies they'd been told.

That, and she wanted him to see them.

She reached for her laptop, opening and unlocking it, pulling up a search window and turning it to him. "There's excellent Wi-Fi out here."

"The sheep riot if they don't have it," he deadpanned, setting his fingers to the keyboard and typing her name.

She tried to stay still. Tried to pretend she didn't have to see the results of his search. But she was only human and he was about to stare into her soul, so what was a girl to do?

Lilah got up and rounded the table, doing her best not to grab the computer and curate the images he saw. Show him the ones she knew were best. Instead, she pressed herself back to the heavy wooden chopping block at the center of the kitchen, and watched over his shoulder as he scrolled.

Scroll scroll *pause.*

Scroll scroll *pause* . . . on an image that had been cropped by some website and now looked awful.

She bit her tongue, willing him to keep going, and when he did, she watched his strong fingers work the trackpad on the laptop. Her attention fell to the Breguet chronograph on his wrist, recognition coming with no small amount of surprise. She'd photographed enough celebrities styled to the teeth to know that the watch easily ran twenty thousand dollars. Apparently there were some perks to working for a duke.

"I've seen some of these before," he said.

She didn't know what to say to that, and she didn't want small talk about the work. She wanted to know what he thought of it. So Lilah held her tongue and watched his face.

"I know this woman," he said, pointing to a stark black-and-white portrait—a woman standing alone outside the marriage bureau at City Hall in Little Rock, Arkansas, a proud glint in her dark eyes.

"VM Mathers," she clarified. The author of *Self Love*, a

book that had spoken to every woman who had ever been with the wrong person and vowed to seize her own destiny. "I took that one a few months after the book came out."

He nodded, recognizing the name. "What's she like?"

Lilah smiled. "Not what you'd expect from a self-help juggernaut. Badass. She took me to the best barbecue of my life immediately after I got that shot."

It was the last shoot Lilah had done before the one that had ruined her.

"And this one . . . Ian Hale—why do I know this one?"

"I don't know," she said. "You don't seem like the kind of person who subscribes to lifestyle magazines." She took a step forward, not trusting herself to get close enough to take over his browsing. "That was my first *Bonfire* cover. I was sick to my stomach showing up for it—I wanted to do something different than shirtless-action-hero-leaning-on-a-rusted-out-car." She paused, then added, "Celebrities often have their own ideas of how they want to be photographed, and they're usually pretty banal and terrible. I knew there was a better-than-even chance he would hear my ideas and storm out."

"And did he?" The words were low and gruff, like he might hunt Ian Hale down if he had been rude to Lilah.

She shouldn't like that, but she did. "No. He was great."

Max had enlarged the photo—the cover. A flawless shot. One that revealed more of Ian Hale than any of the dozens of covers he'd been on before or since. She was proud of that one.

Max grunted his reply and for a heartbeat Lilah wondered at the sound—was it possible he was *jealous*?

"And this one—I remember this picture of the American president."

Half the newspapers in the world had run it on Inauguration Day—the president of the United States, head bowed, framed against nothing but blue sky. "I remember every second of that day. The first woman president, and she wanted me to take the portrait." She shook her head, still in awe. "A thousand other photographers to choose from, and there I was."

"Not a thousand. None like you," he said, softly, drawing her attention.

She met his eyes. "No," she said, the word as much an agreement as it was a reminder to herself. Of who she'd been then. Of who she might still be. "None like me."

"You love it."

I do. She loved the excitement and the people and the knowledge that she could capture a moment that would show *everything* and only because she was astute enough to see everything first.

She loved it, and she wanted it back.

Looking at the screen—her entire past laid out in a mosaic of thumbnails—she was consumed with emotion. She'd worked so hard. She'd done everything right. She'd done magnificent work.

And now . . .

"Nine days," she said, softly.

"Not long," he replied.

Nine days, and she was on a train to London. Away from this place that had somehow already begun to feel like more than a holiday.

Away from this man—his whiskey-colored eyes and his rugged face and his beautiful mouth, set in a firm line that might have been disappointment if she let herself think about it. But she didn't want to think about disappointing him—this man who had impossibly begun to feel like more than a holiday himself.

He closed the laptop and stood, turning to face her. "More than one night though."

Her heart began to pound. "We passed the one-night mark when you went and collected fresh eggs, I think."

He didn't laugh at the joke, instead closing the distance between them. "How many more will you give me?"

She swallowed at the direct question, her lips falling open in surprise. "You don't mess around."

"You leave in nine days, Lilah. I don't have time to mess around." His hands came to cup her face, tilting her up to him. "Nine days, and you go back to your world. To the glitz and the glamour and the parties and the pictures."

She was losing herself in him. In his beautiful eyes. In the rumble of his voice that made her forget what it was she was so desperate to get back to. "Yes."

"Nine days," he repeated, stealing her lips in a soft, lush kiss. "I want them."

Yes.

He was kissing her again, hot and lingering. "Give them to me." She opened her eyes to find him watching her. "Let me spend the days making you laugh and the nights making you come."

This man was absolutely a marauder. "Yes."

With a growl, he walked her back to a clean section of the counter and lifted her up to sit on it, his hands already divesting her of her clothes. Not that she was complaining.

"I thought you had plans for the day?"

"Mmm," he rumbled at her ear, the sound like sin. "They've changed."

7

They spent the next two days living on sex and sleep and whatever they could throw together to eat before they started all over again, and Max did his best to discover every bit of Lilah's glorious body, memorizing the places that made her sigh and the ones that made her laugh and the ones that made her moan.

He liked those the most.

On the third morning, as the early afternoon sun turned the grass in the north pasture the perfect autumn gold, he made good on his original plans, and took Lilah to the folly, Atlas leading the way. At some point after the morning she'd agreed to give him her time at Salterton Abbey, he'd gone to fetch the sheepdog, who seemed as happy to linger with Lilah as Max was.

And he was happy to linger with her, he thought as they crossed the estate in the direction of the tower at the northern edge of the land.

Happy to pull her close and pretend she needed help navigating the collection of stones that would become a brook in the spring.

Happy to thread his fingers through hers as they climbed the small hill just to the north.

Happy to stand back and watch her turn in a circle there, taking in the estate, reaching to retrieve her camera from the bag she'd slung over her shoulder before they'd left the house.

He could have watched her for hours, taking pictures of the land, of the mottled sunlight across the patchwork fields, of the storm clouds on the horizon, of the sheep in the pastures beyond.

And as he watched, it occurred to him that it was he who should have taken photos. Lilah who should have been the subject.

Because in six days she would be gone, and he would have nothing but the memory of her here, with him. And it didn't matter how happy he was here and now—it didn't matter how happy they both were, even as he watched the gleam of pure joy and contentment in her rich brown eyes.

This happiness, like all happiness in Max's experience, was temporary.

At least this time, he'd known it from the start. He'd never expected Lilah to stay, and he could not afford to let himself believe she might. That way lay bitter disappointment, he'd learned that years ago. It was a lesson he'd do well to remember now as the sight of Lilah looking so peaceful and at home on the land that was his birthright and his legacy tempted and threatened.

Six more days, he promised himself. And he'd be damned if he gave up a single moment of them.

Lilah raised her camera, looking through the viewfinder at the estate house rising up on a hill in the distance, far enough away to settle it into the landscape and still imposing enough to give pause.

"You know, I think you can get that exact shot in the gift shop."

She looked up instantly. "Excuse me, you can absolutely *not* get my exact shot in the gift shop."

He laughed at her affront. "I beg your pardon."

"You'd better," she said, feigning seriousness before looking back at the house. "How many rooms are there?"

"One hundred and forty."

"Good lord."

It was ridiculous. "The family lives in about twenty of them. The rest is open to the public."

She nodded, returning to their walk. "I took the tour."

His brows shot up. "You did?"

"I did! The morning after we met."

"I could have given you a tour," he said, suddenly embarrassed and frustrated that she'd been in his home and he hadn't known.

Neither had she.

Embarrassed and frustrated and *guilty*.

"You didn't exactly bring me a basket of baked goods when I arrived, Max."

"I saved you from Mabel."

"Okay, first, I think Mabel and I would have worked it out," she said with a laugh. "And second, I'm guessing that the lovely elderly woman who gave the tour probably knew more about the portrait gallery than you did."

The portrait gallery filled with portraits of his ancestors.

"Although she *really* wanted to talk about the duke."

He snapped his head around to look at her. "She did?"

"Oh yes. According to Judy, not only is he a billionaire, he's *quite dishy and unmarried*."

She said the last in a perfectly theatrical British accent. Max's cheeks warmed. "Mmm."

Lilah waved a hand in the air. "Unfortunately for all of us sad singletons, however, he's also *very secretive* and nursing a *legendary broken heart*."

"What rubbish," he scoffed. Who was this Judy woman?

She shrugged. "I don't know, I thought it was a pretty nice way of getting around the fact that he probably loathes having to mix with the masses. She really sold it. I confess, I was about ready to go Lizzie Benneting around to see if I could find him in the lake."

Right. He wouldn't sack Judy.

"Careful," he said. "If you found me in the lake, I'd do more than Mr. Darcy you."

She turned a delicious smile on him. "Promises, promises."

He kissed her, lingering at that smile. "Unfortunately, we don't have a lake handy."

She shook a head. "What even is the point of having an English country house if you don't have a lake?"

"I don't know. You should ask Judy the next time you take the tour."

"Okay, I give," she said, threading her arm through his. "Regale me with tales of Salterton Abbey."

"What do you want to know?"

"You have an apartment in the main house?"

"I do." *Tell her.*

Tell her, and lose every moment of those six days of happiness.

"You see? And Judy said *nothing* about the hot farmhand."

"Land steward, actually," he corrected. It was the truth. Just not all of it. "But let's get back to me being hot."

"No. If we do that, I'll never see the folly."

That much was true.

"What's it like living in something . . . Versailles-sized?"

He turned wide, affronted eyes on her "Versailles! Please. Balmoral. Windsor. But not *French*."

She laughed, bright and beautiful. "I'm so sorry to offend. Please don't tell your boss. I wouldn't want him to kick me out."

He resisted the urge to flinch. "He wouldn't, you know."

"I'm happy to hear it," she retorted. "Do you know how hard it is to find a good hotel room on short notice? I'd have to convince Simon to let me stay at the Fox and Falcon."

"First, you are *not* staying anywhere near Simon."

Her brows rose. "What's wrong with Simon?"

"He's a bounder and a cad," he said without hesitation. "And besides, you're allowed to stay as long as you wish."

"Even if the duke knew I compared his castle to Versailles?"

"Even then."

"Ah. He's the good kind of duke, then?"

He looked away. "He tries to be."

Except for now. He can't seem to be the good kind of man right now. Not when it means losing the pleasure you've promised him.

They walked in silence for a while, waving to a young family who had come to the estate for a wander. An older girl was attempting to teach a little one how to do a cartwheel, and Lilah slowed to look, giving Max time to watch her.

To wonder what it would be like if she were his to watch, always.

When the little one toppled over almost instantly, Lilah chuckled, and the woman with them looked over with a smile and a shrug.

"I like that the estate is public," Lilah said as they resumed their journey.

"I do too." Max waved to the family from a distance. "I like that it belongs to residents of and visitors to Salterton as much as to the title," he said, repeating his father's words, repeated from his grandfather.

"But not to photographers," she said, teasing.

One side of his mouth lifted. "We make an exception for hot ones."

She grinned. "So I'm hot now, too?"

"Shall I show you how much?"

He reached for her, but she slipped from his fingers with a laugh. "No deal, Lancelot. I was promised a folly. Tell me more. You've lived here your whole life, you said."

"Yes." *The truth.*

"Family business?"

"Mmm," he said, hating the non-answer.

She shook her head. "Wild. And you never thought about leaving?"

"I did leave, for a while."

She understood instantly. "The fallen-apart marriage."

"The very same."

They walked for a bit longer, and Max was grateful that Lilah didn't pull away from him. He wanted to tell her this truth—even if he didn't want to tell her all of it.

And she waited for him.

"We were young and in love," he started, surprising himself with the words. "But I'd lived here my whole life and she'd spent her life in London. She didn't want sheep and hay and lazy evenings down the pub. And I didn't want the city, the parties, the people." He'd never told anyone the rest. "I thought I could love her enough to get her to stay.

And Georgiana thought she could love me enough to get me to leave."

She nodded. "You were on different paths."

Just as we are.

He'd seen the longing on her face when she'd talked about her work in that world—Christ, she'd taken photos of presidents and princes and superstars—and he could see how much she wanted to get back to it every time she lifted her camera to her eye.

Could see, too, that someone had taken it from her. He'd seen that look before on a woman he loved. Disappointment and sadness and something worse. *Regret.*

He'd never be someone's regret again.

Lilah would never have cause to regret Max. She would leave in less than a week, none the wiser as to his title, and he would remain a lovely, satisfying interlude in her long and interesting life—a happy memory. He could hope for that. He could be that.

Because she *would* leave. And he would stay. And that was where this story ended.

"How long were you married?"

He looked out toward the tower, just visible at the center of a copse of trees on the next rise. "We met at eighteen. Married at twenty-three. Divorced at twenty-six."

"Wow," she said, softly.

"My greatest failure," he said.

"Please. You were young and in love and believed it was enough. We all do stupid things for love at twenty-three."

He looked at her, appreciating the matter-of-fact way she said it. Like it was true. "What did you do?"

"I went to *art school*, Max. About the only stupid thing I *didn't* do is get married to the wrong person, and honestly that was only because I was falling for a different wrong person every week."

The confession freed Max. "And do you still do that?"

"What, fall for the wrong person?"

"Mmm."

"Ask me in six days," she teased, not looking at him. Instead, she took in the wide expanse of Weston lands, but Max missed the vista with its enormous rolls of baled hay dotting the fields, lush wood in a riot of color, and the house itself in the distance.

He was too busy watching Lilah, more breathtaking than the land beyond.

"Growing up here must have been amazing," she said, pulling him from his thoughts.

"It was," he agreed. "Summers, when we were home from school—Simon and I . . . we'd spend every minute of daylight exploring."

She smiled. "Bounders and cads in training?"

"He was the bounder and cad."

"And you? Scoundrel and rogue?"

"In training. How did I do?"

She tilted her head. "Terrible."

"I shall endeavor to try harder."

"See that you do," she said before adding, "And what about other kinds of friends?"

He slid her a look. "What other kinds of friends?"

"Girls, Max," she said, as though speaking to a small child. "What about girls?"

They were nearing the top of the rise, closing in on a cluster of trees that had been there for two hundred years. "I'm familiar with the concept."

She laughed. "I bet you were a heartbreaker."

"I did all right."

"Tell me about your first kiss."

He stopped in his tracks. "I most certainly will not."

She burst out laughing. "That was the most British you've ever sounded! Are you afraid you'll ruin her reputation?"

"A gentleman would never."

Lilah grinned. "Surely there's a statute of limitations on kissing and telling."

"How long would you say that is?"

"Twenty years," she said, all certainty.

"Fair enough. Her name was Claire, we were ten, and it was very fast because we were absolutely certain we were about to be discovered by the vicar."

"The vicar!"

"The vicar. We only ever saw each other after services on Sunday mornings."

She made a show of looking shocked. "Kissing behind the church hedgerow is scandalous, Max."

"It wasn't behind the hedgerow; it was in the graveyard."

Lilah's pretend shock disappeared. "Wow. I'm honestly impressed. And a little jealous. My first kiss was in the back row of my high school auditorium with Brock D'Avino during rehearsal for the school musical."

"Young Brock deserved a talking to, no doubt."

"Well, I can't remember anything about him but his name, so I don't think it was very memorable. The point is, it wasn't anywhere near as interesting as a *graveyard*."

He winced. "Don't say it like that. Makes it seem really grim."

"Sunday morning cemetery snogging is better?"

"I wouldn't exactly call it a snog."

"Chaste smooching."

He chuckled. "Better."

They walked for a bit longer, and Lilah asked, "So, what happened to Claire?"

"Living quite happily in London with her partner and twin girls, last I heard."

"Too bad."

He cut her a look. "Not so bad." Suddenly, nothing in his past felt bad. None of it could, if it had led him here, to this. To her, beautiful and fresh-faced and him, here, now. If just for a moment. And if six days of her was all he ever got, it would be enough.

Lie.

She stilled, pulling him around to face her, and he read the understanding in her eyes. The desire in them—a desire he recognized because it was his as well. "No," she agreed, softly. "Not bad at all."

She came up on her toes to meet him as he dipped his head and they kissed, and he didn't want it to stop, soft and sweet and full of pleasure.

When they broke apart, Lilah's eyes remained closed for a heartbeat, and Max took the moment to drink her in, warm and sun-kissed, a dusting of freckles across her cheeks, where her dark lashes lay. And then she whispered, "If I'm not careful, I'm going to like you more than six days' worth."

He already liked her too much.

He swallowed the realization, grateful that they'd arrived at their destination. The little tower stood a few yards away now that they were at the top of the ridge. Clearing his throat, he waved a hand in its direction. "The folly. As requested."

8

It was perfect. A little stone tower, complete with arched windows and a rooftop parapet, made to look like a tiny medieval castle out here in the middle of nowhere.

Lilah let out a little gasp of excitement. "Can we go in?"

"Of course. What good would it be otherwise?"

She didn't need to be told twice. There was nothing inside—the small door led to a staircase, winding around a great central column to the roof. In the doorway, she turned back to Max, still outside, still watching her. "Are you coming?"

He followed as she made her way up the winding stairs, catching up to her when she stilled on the small platform halfway up the tower to look out the tall, narrow opening there, the breeze whispering through the arch, cool and crisp. Atlas was already bounding off into the distance, released from herding humans for a while.

She lifted her camera and took a picture a thousand other people must have taken. She didn't care. It wasn't for the world. It was for her.

To bring her back, when it was over.

"The view is better from the top," Max said, the low rumble curling through her.

He was right.

Coming through the small doorway at the top of the turret, Lilah walked to the edge, nothing in the world able to stop her. Camera in hand, she set her bag down at the base of the tower wall, peeking over, surveying the land. "This is like the greatest tree house ever. Did you play here as a kid?"

"It's an excellent hiding place, if you are ever looking for one. Visitors never come this far north, and everyone on the estate forgets it exists."

She shook her head. "England is real wild."

He laughed. "Americans love a castle."

"And what's wrong with that?" she tossed over her shoulder. "I, for one, feel like the heroine in a romance novel," she said. "Out on the ramparts, watching for soldiers coming home from battle."

"Mmm," he said, wrapping an arm around her waist and pressing a kiss at the place where her neck met her shoulder. "I like the idea of coming home from battle to you."

She turned in his arms as his touch and words warmed her. "Mmm," she repeated, teasing. "Maybe I'd like to come home from battle to *you* on the ramparts."

"Waiting to warm you by the fire?" His tongue swirled against her pulse. "No. We go to war together."

"Sword in your sheath, blade in my kirtle?" She sighed.

"Sounds proper filthy. Let's do it."

She laughed and pulled away from him, finding the sunlight on his face, his eyes bright and warm with pleasure and teasing, and the sound trailed off. "My God, Max. You're so pretty."

He dipped his chin at the words, and she loved that she'd embarrassed him.

"Let me take your picture."

His attention immediately returned to her, his brow furrowed, like he didn't know what to say.

"I'll be gentle," she said with a smile. "You won't feel a thing."

He laughed and rubbed a hand back and forth at the back of his neck. "I don't know anything about being a model."

She shook her head. "No modeling necessary. I just want—"

I want to remember you.

Lilah swallowed around the thought, hating the tightness in her chest. "I just want to take a picture of you, here. With the land you work behind you. With the sun that loves you on your skin."

"Only if I am able to take a picture of you at the end."

"You drive a hard bargain, but I accept. And you will be very, very disappointed to know that I do *not* photograph well."

"I don't believe it."

"It's true," she said, lifting the Nikon, watching him in the viewfinder as she joked, "Mine's the kind of beauty that moves."

He laughed.

Click.

"I wasn't ready."

"You were perfect," she said, immediately reframing.

He hesitated.

Don't blink.

There.

Click.

"*You're* perfect," he said.

The words sent a shot of pure pleasure through her. She lowered the camera, wanting to remember this moment, his eyes on her, seeing her in a way no one had ever seen her. She swallowed, her heart pounding. She was excited. Nervous.

Photographing Max, here, felt like she was taking pictures for the first time.

"Are you sure you don't model on the side, farmhand?"

"I've been practicing for my new Instagram account."

Click. That sly smile.

She laughed. "Too few piglets."

Click. And the easy one, like home.

Click. Watching her. Not posing.

"You love this."

On autopilot, Lilah readjusted her grip, moving with the light, backing away. Considering the angle of the shadows behind him as they lengthened in the afternoon sun. "It's all I've ever wanted to do. Since I was a kid and my dad dug an old Polaroid camera out of a box in the attic and let me have it." She paused. "Did you ever play with one of those?"

Click. Memory.

"I don't think we ever had one."

"I loved them. The picture would appear like it was coming through fog. It felt like magic. My dad bought up as much instant film as he could find at yard sales and thrift shops. And I took about twelve thousand pictures of the cat."

Click. The handsomest of grins.

"How old were you?"

"Seven or eight," she said, lowering the camera. "After the cat, I turned to portraits. My parents, my friends, my teachers, strangers. We took a summer vacation to the Outer

Banks and I convinced a dozen people in line for ice cream to let me photograph them." She shook her head, stuck in the memory. "My poor mother. She didn't know what to do with me. But I still remember that when we developed that roll of film—she turned to me and said, in her thickest Georgia drawl, 'Well, Lilah Rose, I suppose you're going to be an *artist*.'"

"They were good?"

"They would have been better if I'd been able to develop them myself, but my mom vetoed turning the downstairs bathroom into a darkroom for some reason." She lifted the Nikon. "They bought me my first digital camera for my next birthday, and no one in my life was safe."

"Not even me," he said.

"Especially not you. Too many good angles."

"You like my angles, do you?"

The teasing question coiled through her as her focus narrowed on him, tall and broad in the golden light. "I might need a better look."

That smile. So easy. Max spread his arms wide. "I present myself to the artist for inspection."

Yum.

She turned away for a heartbeat, just enough time to set her camera back in her bag. Max had relaxed against the parapet wall again, a modern-day knight. His arms were stretched across the edge, the collar of his navy blue sweater unzipped to reveal a hint of sun-kissed skin. He wore the same Chameaus from their first meeting—crossed one over the other like he had all the time in the world for her blatant appraisal.

"Applying for position of muse?" She approached, slow and deliberate. When she was close enough to touch him, she stopped, drinking him in. Shadows and light, hard lines and smooth edges.

"If you'll have me," he said, the words rough like stone.

She went heavy with want and stepped closer, setting her hands to his chest, tracing the lines of him, the sinew of his strong arms stretched out across the wall, the ridges of muscles down over his chest and abdomen, beneath his sweater. She slid her fingers beneath the hem, searching for the warm skin of his waist, and he sucked in a breath at the touch of her cold hands.

"It's difficult to decide," she said, unable to keep the need from her words. "With all these clothes."

"Mmm."

She loved that sound. When this was over, that low rumble would follow her forever. She'd summon it on late nights, in the dark, when she let herself remember this week, slipped out of time.

Pushing the thought of *over* out of the way, Lilah stroked one hand down the outside of his trousers, finding his cock hard beneath the fabric.

"Visitors never get this far north?"

His eyes went liquid with heat and understanding. "Everyone forgets it exists."

Lilah rewarded the words by tracing the ridge of him, heavy and thick, and delighting in his low groan, in the way her touch undid him. She leaned in and pressed a lingering, soft kiss to the skin at the open collar of his shirt. "May I?"

He swore, and she took it as a yes.

"Hands stay on the wall, please," she whispered in his ear before she traced her lips across his jaw, down the column of his neck, the slide mimicked by another, lower, his trousers opening, releasing the swell of his cock into her waiting hands.

"Lilah," he whispered. "You're going to kill me."

"Mmm," she said, still playing her part, pulling the fabric down and revealing the stunning, straining length of him. Her mouth watered as she stroked over him, reveling in the feel of him, hot and hard. She couldn't help her whisper, "Look at this gorgeous cock."

"Fuck, yes," he said, harsh. "Look at it."

Her gaze flickered up to his, finding him staring at her. She fisted him, stroking from base to tip, loving the way the movement wrecked him, his eyes going hooded, his chest rumbling with a low growl of pleasure. "I don't just want to look at it, Max."

His eyes narrowed and he leaned down, not taking his hands from the wall even as he claimed her mouth—ever the marauder—tongue delving deep, stroking over hers until she gasped with pleasure.

"Whatever you want, love."

Love.

She ignored the way the word rioted through her, filling her with a wave of pleasure, leaving her hot and heavy with need, instead returning her attention to him, tracing ridges and veins, "I want it all."

"Christ," he said, "I can see how much you want it. Fuck, you're beautiful—" She stroked him again, and his words were lost in a groan as his hips rocked against her touch.

"You like that," she whispered.

"I like that very much," he said with a laugh. "I like *you*. Kiss me again."

She did, heat pooling at her core, making her ache in the best possible way. As she continued to work him over, fucking him with her hands, memorizing the length and feel of him, his thick shaft and the beautiful pink head of him, moist with the evidence of his need for her.

"Fuck, Lilah, you look . . . "

She could see it. She could see how she looked in his eyes. On his face. "Hungry," she whispered. "I'm hungry, Max."

She slid to her knees in front of him, and he gritted his teeth, the muscles of his jaw working as she knew he did all he could not to touch her, this gorgeous man, giving himself up to her whims. God, he was perfect.

This is perfect, she thought as she stroked him, loving the way his strong, lean hips met her movements, and she watched, feeling the straining steel of him, reveling in his size as she looked up at him, in the cords of his neck and the clench of his jaw and the white-knuckled grip he kept on the parapet wall because she'd told him to.

She rewarded them both, licking over the tip of him, salty sweetness exploding on her tongue as his curse exploded in her ears, one hand coming off the wall, uncontrollable, threading into her hair, tightening in her curls until she groaned too, at the delicious sting of his touch.

And somehow this glorious man didn't move, even as she teased him, keeping his pleasure from him. From her, even as his cock throbbed in her hand and his breath hung between them, ragged and uneven.

"You want to fuck me, don't you?" she said to the straining length of him, knowing she tempted fate.

"No," he bit out, summoning her surprise. She looked up at him, meeting his eyes, his pupils blown with need. "I want you to fuck me."

The words were her pleasure and her power.

And then he added, "But I want you to fuck yourself too."

She stilled.

His pleasure. His power.

"I want you to spread your legs and slide your fingers beneath your clothes, and tell me how wet you are." He slid one booted foot between her knees, helping her widen them. "Go on, beautiful."

She did as she was told, her fingers sliding over her pussy, her breath catching with the pleasure of her own touch.

"That's it," he said, encouraging her even as she could hear the way everything about this moment was wrecking him. Wrecking them both. "Find the place where it aches, love."

She did, her eyelids flickering when she stroked over her clit.

"There it is," he whispered. "Are you wet for me?"

She nodded.

"Mmm."

Wetter for him now.

He used his fist in her hair to tilt her up to him. "Are you sure you don't want me to do it? Sure you don't want me to lay you down here in the sunlight on this tower and eat you until you scream? I want that," he said. "I want the taste of you on me all day, sex and sin."

He was destroying her. She did want that.

But she wanted him more. "No," she said, loving the surprise in his eyes when she leaned forward and licked the underside of him, long and lingering and wet, until she reached the tip of him. "I want this."

And she parted her lips and took him in, loving the heavy slide over her tongue, the salty fire that came with it, the hard heat of him. The way he let out a long, slow breath as she drew him deep, one hand stroking over his shaft, reveling in his ragged breath and his filthy words as he reached for control.

As she unraveled him. The pace, the pressure, the places that made him wild, summoning more of those deep-throated rumbles.

"Don't stop," he whispered, looking down at her, drawing her attention to his face.

She wasn't going to stop; she wanted everything from him.

She took him deep, and his fist tightened again, slowing her movements. "*Don't stop*," he bit out. "Make yourself come."

The words set her on fire, and she fucked them both, taking him in long, lush strokes, again and again, over and over, and stroking herself, wet and wanting, until she had to focus on one of them, and of course it would be him—because his pleasure was hers, the sounds he made, the filthy words he whispered as she found the rhythm that was his undoing, until finally, the hand he'd kept on the wall came to her hair, stroking soft and reverent and he groaned, "Lilah, love, if you—I'm going to—"

Yes. She willed him. *Give it to me.*

He grew, impossibly harder, impossibly thicker against her tongue, pulsing against her.

She took him deep and he came, shouting her name, loud and rough and devastating, to the land and the sky and this tower that she would never forget, salt and musk and Max, her hands stroking up his thighs, over the trembling muscles of his stomach as his touch gentled and he caught his breath.

She stayed with him until he returned to himself, easing himself from her lips, and Lilah sat back on her heels, looking up at him as the expression on his face moved from pure pleasure to something that looked more than a little dangerous.

Her eyes widened as he yanked up his trousers, ignoring the fastenings on them, and came to his own knees before her, reaching for her, pulling her in for a deep, intense kiss. When it was over, he growled against her lips. "I said *don't stop.*"

"I was busy," she replied.

"Mmm. Well, it looks like I'm going to have to take matters into my own hands."

She squealed as he flipped her back, reaching beneath her sweater to pull her jeans down past her knees, locking her ankles together as he spread her thighs and wedged his broad shoulders between them. "Max—" she started, but there was nothing more to say, the rest of the words forgotten with the pleasure of his mouth, hard and urgent against her.

"You taste like the fucking sun," he said, lifting his head for a heartbeat, just long enough to slide his hands beneath her ass and tilt her up to him, like a banquet.

Like she was a feast.

And God, he feasted, his tongue thick and perfect, licking over her, rubbing back and forth over her clit, where she ached for release, again and again, faster and faster until *her* fingers were tight in his hair and she was rocking against him, crying out, "Please, Max."

"Mmm."

That growl, that deep rumble, combined with a thick finger, stroking deep, just there . . . just enough . . . She came hard, shouting his name to the sky. And this time Max held her while she returned to thought, restoring her clothing and rolling to his back and pulling her into his arms, holding her tight against him as her breath returned and her heartbeat resumed a normal rhythm.

They lay there in easy silence, at the top of the folly, for what seemed like hours, the sunlight spilling through the ancient trees, and Lilah traced the shadows of the leaves on his chest, willing time to stop, just for a bit. Just for a few more days.

Just until he wasn't so perfect.

"I didn't get my pictures," he said after a while.

She smiled. "You got something better though, no?"

Silence. And then, "I still want the picture."

Warmth threaded through her, and she shifted, reaching into the back pocket of her jeans to extract her phone.

"Don't trust me with the real thing?" Max said, teasing.

"This one is better for Instagram," she quipped, flipping the camera and handing it to him. "You've got a longer arm," she said, tucking herself against him, adjusting the angle of his reach to avoid shadows, framing the shot with precision.

"You can take the photography away from the girl . . . " Max intoned, his lips curved as he watched her on the screen.

"Hush," she said. "Take the picture."

He turned and kissed her temple.

Don't blink, Lilah. You might miss it.

9

Max and Lilah lingered on the estate, exploring until the sun had almost set and Atlas had to lead them home through the fast-darkening fields, as Max lit the last bit of the journey with the flash-light on his phone.

They tumbled into the cottage like young lovers sneaking home after curfew, cheeks red from the evening chill, and Lilah scraped together pickle and ham and cheese and a packet of Ryvita while he built a fire in the study. After supper, he poured them both a Scotch and they curled together beneath a cashmere blanket he'd unearthed, Atlas by the fire.

Max watched as Lilah pulled up the shots from the folly and proved to him that she was one of the greatest portrait photographers the world had ever seen.

"Here," she'd said, finally finished editing the picture she'd deemed the best of the bunch, one where he looked happy and relaxed on the land. "Let me send you this one. They should put it on the Salterton Abbey website."

He pressed a kiss to her temple and said, "I don't care about the one of me. Where's the one of us?"

With a little laugh, she snatched up her phone from the low table nearby and pulled up the picture. "You know, there was a time when many, many people in the world would have done crime for a portrait session with me. And you want the selfie."

"I want the one with you."

She fiddled with it, opening the edit menu to play with lighting and crop it just so, and he watched, marveling at the idea that anyone could take so long perfecting a photo they'd snapped with a phone.

When she was done, she sent it to him, and they returned to what she called *farmhouse idyll.*

And it felt like idyll, like time had stopped, the world no longer beyond the windows now that her ear was pressed to his chest, the warm weight of her like a gift as he told her about the estate—about goats on the rough land to the west, the sheep in the east pasture, the beehives that would have to be wintered soon.

As she told him stories of the farmers she'd met on her travels—the apiarist in Crete, the cattle crowdfarming initiative in Ghana, the women dry-growing grapes on California's Central Coast.

And it was not lost on either of them that it was perfect.

Or that it was fleeting.

When the fire waned, left to nothing but embers, Max took the empty glass from Lilah's hand and guided her off the couch and up the stairs to bed, where he stripped her bare and lay her down and reset the clock once more, worshipping her long and slow, like they had all the time in the world.

Of course, they didn't have all the time in the world, but neither of them wanted to think about that.

Not that night, with six days ahead of them like a promise. And not the next.

But it became more and more difficult for Max to think about giving her up at the end of their time together. And more and more difficult to hold his tongue when all he wanted to do was beg her to stay.

He'd fallen for her.

It wasn't supposed to have happened. It was supposed to have been nine days—nine days of easy companionship and intense pleasure. Nine days in isolation, without either of them knowing enough about the other to complicate things.

Nine days with Max and Lilah, and no one else.

She didn't know the truth of who he was, and he didn't know the truth of what she'd run from, and every time he thought to tell her or ask her, he resisted, because it was only supposed to be nine days, long and lush and free.

But they weren't free anymore. Because Max didn't want to be free of her.

Wild as it seemed after not even a week, he'd fallen for this woman, and he wanted a shot at forever with her. But forever meant more than Max and Lilah in a cottage tucked away deep in the Devon countryside.

Forever meant real life. It meant the Duke of Weston hermited away at his estate, and Lilah Rose, celebrity photographer and friend of the glitterati in New York and Paris and Hollywood or wherever.

Except she had stopped. She'd left that world for a time. Something had happened, and he'd never pressed her on it. *I didn't know if I'd ever be able to take pictures again*. She'd sold her studio. Disappeared.

Why?

And so, as they lay in bed, tired and sated from another round of the best sex he'd ever had, and likely would ever have, her fingers trailing through the hair on his chest, his tracing patterns over her soft skin, the scent of her filling him like sunshine, he asked her.

"Why did you stop?"

"Stop what?" The reply was full of sleepy satisfaction, and Max nearly didn't clarify. He didn't want to burst the bubble.

But he had to know whether the future was an option.

"Your work. Posh photography."

She stilled against him. "You don't think sheep are posh?"

"Hey," he said, softly, and she lifted her head to look at him. "You don't ever have to use your armor with me."

She watched him for a long moment, and then put her head back to his chest. "I want to believe that."

He waited, willing her to speak. Knowing he couldn't ask her to tell him anything. Knowing she didn't owe him truth. Knowing he didn't deserve it.

And then, "I turned down the wrong man."

Every muscle in his body tensed, and he went hot with immediate anger. "What does that mean?"

She didn't look at him. "I was asked to shoot a cover for *Culture Magazine*. They were doing a huge piece on a very powerful man." No name. Max gritted his teeth, going through the dozens of possibilities. "It was massive—ten thousand words, the first of its kind about someone the whole world knew and, it seemed, no one knew."

More likely, someone everyone knew, and no one was willing to discuss. Max was a member of the British aristocracy—they'd practically invented sweeping scandal under the rug.

Lilah took a deep breath, her body pressing closer to his, as though she needed strength to go on. "To get the story, the editor-in-chief of *Culture* had made a number of promises. The subject got to choose his interviewer, location, approve a list of staff and colleagues who would be the only people *Culture* could contact."

Fury flared. "And you."

She nodded. "I wanted the gig. I'd worked with the magazine before. I liked the team there. They respected me . . . or so I thought. So I didn't really think twice. He chose the photographer for the piece . . . and the location, date and time for the shoot."

Max cursed, low and dark, his hand going wide over her shoulder, tight, as though he could protect her in hindsight.

"It's funny, how you see it. I didn't. I should have known when they said they were willing to triple my fee. I'm not exactly cheap to begin with. But I was at the top of my game, and hubris is real."

No. Whatever this story—however it played out, it wasn't her fault. "Lilah—"

She cut him off before he could argue. "I'd shot the *Bonfire* Hollywood issue earlier in the year and I had the Finezzi Calendar scheduled. This cover—it would be a hat trick." She paused and looked up at him. "A hat trick is when—"

"I know. It comes from cricket."

"It does? Cool." She smiled and he would have matched it if he wasn't resisting the urge to book a flight immediately to wherever this man was and do damage.

"Lilah . . . "

"He chose his house in the Hamptons. His wife would be there, his staff, his kids, probably. But if I came in the evening, things would be quieter. Would that be fine?"

"Fucking hell." Not damage. He'd do murder.

"I drove out from the city," she said. "I borrowed a friend's car—this nonsense convertible that half the time wouldn't even start—but it was a beautiful spring day and I spent the drive out going over the ideas that I'd had for the shoot. His staff had sent me photos of this mansion—it was bananas. All white walls and chrome and steel and built right on the edge of the Atlantic. I'd been in houses like it before—it was my job not to be impressed. But this house —" She quieted. "Well. It was bananas."

"He was alone."

She nodded. "He was used to photographers, but not artists, he told me, and he thought it would be easier if it was just the two of us. Gross, right?" She paused. "I really thought it would be fine. I'd dealt with slimeballs before." Max growled, and she looked at him with amused surprise. "What was that?"

"Me, resisting the urge to ask you to make me a list."

She let out a little laugh, like he had made a joke. It wasn't a joke. It was truth. This story was turning him into pure vengeance, and he probably shouldn't like it but he was too busy imagining how much he'd enjoy putting his fist into this man's face.

"I handled them just fine," she said, stacking her hands on his chest and setting her chin to them. "Athletes, actors, talk show hosts, princes, every kind of egomaniac you could come up with . . . billionaires are the worst. Here's the thing —they're all the same. They want the power play, but they want the great picture more. So I get in, get the shot, find a way to turn them down, and get out. No problem."

She stopped, the air between them heavy with the story, Max's jaw aching from the clench of his teeth. If this man had hurt her, he would move every mountain he could to punish him. He'd use every inch of the dukedom to ruin him.

"Lilah," he said, her name coming out like gravel. Sounding like he was in pain.

"He didn't touch me," she said quickly, as though to soothe him, and a twist of relief curled through Max, though not enough. He might not have touched her, but she'd been harmed. She'd stopped working, for Christ's sake, and she loved working.

"He went to get something; he claimed to have a folio of unseen Helen Levitt shots that he'd bought at auction—his staff must have done some research, because Helen Levitt is one of the few people who could have made me stick around. Anyway, when he came back, he was naked." She scoffed. "I should've taken a picture of *that*. But I didn't. I took off."

"The car started." There. More relief. More fury.

She gave a little laugh. "Thank God. And I thought it was over. I called my best friend and told her the whole story on the drive back and I still remember coming over the bridge into the city and saying, clear as day, 'But I got the fucking shot.'" She looked at him. "And I did. I had this vision of that shot on the cover of the most respected magazine in the world—revealing what a creep that guy was."

He didn't doubt she'd gotten the shot. Of course she had.

That was her job, and she was remarkable at it.

He stroked his hand down the soft skin of her back, pride warring with a dozen other emotions, not the least of which was fear. The photograph hadn't been enough. Something else had happened. "Then what?"

Sadness clouded her beautiful eyes, and Max's chest tightened. He already hated what was to come. "Three days later I got a call from *Culture*. They were going in a different direction with the story. I'd be paid, but the images wouldn't run. 'Please deliver the files to the magazine and delete any copies.'" She spoke to his chin as he continued to stroke down her spine. Back up. "A few days after that, we got word that *Bonfire* had decided to reshoot the Hollywood issue with a new photographer. A different direction. Literally weeks before the issue shipped. It was unheard of."

Fury threaded through him. Hot and angry and foreign. "And Finezzi?" He didn't know much about the calendar, but he knew it was an enormous win for art photographers.

She shook her head. "Different direction."

"Christ."

"It was going to be great," she said, her eyes meeting his. Max heard the urgency in her voice, as though it was important she say it out loud. And it was the truth. He knew it. It would have been magnificent. He knew, without question, that Lilah Rose would have made sure the whole world knew about that calendar. "I had this plan to play with hard and soft—I wanted to go back to the original erotic pinup style, but really change the gaze. Shoot the whole thing centering women and pleasure and power. Twelve women who were unashamed of passion. Upend the whole thing."

"That sounds perfect," he said. It sounded like exactly the kind of thing this glorious woman would do.

"It would have been. It was the dream, and I could reach out and touch it. And he robbed me of it." There was anger in the words, along with frustration and sadness and fury. She gave a little wave of her hand. "Like that. He robbed me of my career. And the rest of the world helped. My agent—who'd signed me when I was twenty years old and not even out of art school—she stopped calling me. My mentors, who I thought would stand by me. All those people I thought were my friends . . . " She laughed, the sound without humor. "A few months ago, I was in Ghana?"

Max nodded, hating this story and wanting to hear all of it. Every word.

"I pulled out my phone and scrolled through it, and deleted two hundred and seventy-three contacts. Dozens of people who would make you starry-eyed."

"I promise you they wouldn't make me starry-eyed."

She shot him a look. "They make everyone starry-eyed."

He shook his head. "Not me."

After a while, she said, "Weirdly, I believe that."

But it didn't help, he could see. It didn't soothe the furrow at her brow that had come with the memory. He touched that furrow. Smoothed it.

"They were supposed to be my friends," she said, softly, and his heart broke a little bit at the words. "But they didn't care about me. They cared about what I could do for them. Ironically, *Bonfire* ran a piece about me once." She smiled as she remembered the headline. "*Kiss from a Rose.* Lilah Rose, whose photos could turn a star into a supernova."

She shook her head, seeming not to be able to find the right words, and he wanted so much to give them to her. "You weren't just good at it," he said. "You cared about it. You loved it. Your work meant something."

"Yes," she said, softly. "I know what it looks like from the outside. I know it seems frivolous and silly. Who cares about the photograph? We all have cameras in our pockets and we've all taken a decent picture now and then. But I really thought . . . " She trailed off, and Max couldn't bear it. The loss. "I built it. It was mine. I was good at it and I gave up everything for it. No real friends, no real love life, no real life in general. Nothing outside of this one thing that I did well and that I loved. And then . . . it was gone." Her eyes met his. "And then . . . I was gone too."

He ached for her. He ached for what she'd suffered and what she'd lost and for how hard she'd worked and for how hard she fought, still, for this world that should have lowered itself to its knees and thanked the heavens that it had her.

Just as he would lower himself to his knees if he might have her even a fraction as much.

And he ached for himself, for the keen, clear understanding that the only thing she desired was the thing he would never be able to give her.

His silence had stretched too long, until Lilah pulled back from it. "I'm sorry," she said, pushing up off his chest to move away, her eyes gone liquid. "That was a lot."

"No." He rolled with her, cradling her face, running his thumbs over her cheeks, refusing to let her go until he told her exactly what he thought of her. "Thank you," he said. "Thank you for telling me."

She took a deep, shuddering breath. "No problem."

He couldn't help his small smile. She was so strong. "Now I have to tell *you* something."

For an instant, he considered doing it. Telling her his truth, a secret for a secret, and finally having it all out in the open between them. He wanted it so badly, the words burned in his throat—but this moment was not for him. This moment was for Lilah, and what she'd been through, and the fact that she'd shared it with him, and no one else.

He waited for her to look at him. "You are the finest person I know."

Her eyes went liquid with tears.

"No, Lilah." He brushed the hair from her face, searching it, memorizing it. "You are strong and clever and you play darts like a professional, and you are a brilliant artist with—somehow, though I cannot understand how—a spine of pure steel."

"Thank you."

The tears spilled, and he leaned down to kiss her, sipping the words from her lips, before he pulled back and said, "Now. Who was it?"

She exhaled on a laugh. "Why, are you going to go punch his lights out?"

"It's a damn good start."

She reached up and pulled him down for another kiss. "You're really very sweet, you know."

"I'm not feeling very sweet right now." He was feeling murderous right now.

"I can take care of myself. Remember? Blade in my kirtle?"

He didn't rise to the bait. "Save it. Let me bloody my sword instead."

She tilted her head, her gaze narrowing on his. "Why is that so hot?"

"It's not meant to be."

She ran her fingers through his hair and traced the high arc of his cheek and the straight edge of his jaw, still twitching with anger. "I'm already fighting."

He understood, instantly. "Four days."

She nodded. "Four days. I return. And the pictures—they're a good opening salvo."

God, he was so proud of her. "They'll get you what you want."

"The return of Lilah Rose."

Four days. Four days, and she would be gone.

Four days, and Lilah would head back to her glittering life and her glamorous parties, and she would leave Max here and the farmer she'd once known would fade away as she returned to London, or New York, or Los Angeles or whatever place she needed to be.

He'd tried that life before. And he'd ruined a marriage with his inability to love it. He'd disappointed Georgiana, but somehow the idea of disappointing Lilah was worse.

"Max?"

He looked down at her, this woman he loved, strong and clever and so beautiful she made him ache. "Yes?"

"Do you own a suit?"

He froze, knowing what was to come next. Knowing it would be the most difficult thing he'd ever done to reply.

She smiled. God, he loved her smile. "Come to London with me."

He hesitated, and she waited, ever patient.

Yes.

Christ, he wanted to say yes.

But he hadn't fallen for her. He'd fallen in love with her.

The only thing that mattered was her happiness. And he knew, without question, that he could not make her happy. Not forever.

And he couldn't bear the thought of anything less.

"I can't."

10

"I bollocksed it."

Simon considered Max through the small crack in the door of the Fox and Falcon the next morning, before letting him in, wet and bedraggled, Atlas on his heels. Peering out into the torrential rain in the street beyond, the owner of the pub said, "Must have done if you're out in this."

Closing the door, Simon turned to his new guests, wincing when Atlas shook the rain from his coat and went to lie down by the fireplace. "My pub is going to smell like wet dog."

"Think of it as an improvement," Max said before getting to the important bit. "Simon . . . she left."

Simon nodded to a stool at the bar and Max moved to sit. "We knew she was leaving, didn't we? Back to America, no?"

"I had three more days." Max rubbed a hand across his chest, hating the ache there—one he hadn't felt in a lifetime. "We were supposed to have three more days, and she left."

"Because you're naff at women."

"I'm not naff at women."

"All right, I'll play." Simon checked his watch. "Why are you here at twenty past eight in the morning? Instead of abed with your pretty dartsmistress?"

"Because my pretty dartsmistress is gone."

"Because you're naff at women." Simon slipped behind the bar and said, "Pint?"

"It's twenty past eight in the morning, Simon."

"Coffee it is, then." Simon turned away. "So, what, you told her you were duke and she took to the hills, afraid of a long line of aristocratic inbreeding?"

"No."

Simon stilled and turned back. "Shit, Max. You told her you were Duke eventually, didn't you?"

"No," he said. "I didn't think it would matter in the long run. Not if she was leaving. Not if we were just . . ."

Simon stilled. "You didn't think it mattered that you owned the house she was staying in."

The house they were both staying in.

"And half of Devon," his friend added.

Max rubbed his face with both hands, shoving his fingers through his wet hair.

"And a large swath of London."

Christ, he was an ass.

"You didn't think she might like to know that you're one of the richest men in Britain?"

That got Max's attention. Simon and he never talked about the dukedom. They talked about the pub and the sheep and the land, about Lottie's art and Simon's mother's ailments. But they never talked about Max's money.

Simon gave him a half-smile. "You think I grew up in the

back room of this pub, in the shadow of Salterton Abbey, and didn't know that my best friend was rich as royalty? *Richer* than royalty?"

"Christ, Si." Max dipped his head, loathing the conversation. "Come on."

"I didn't invent Google. Take it up with your fellow billionaires. Look. You are a good friend, and a great partner in a brawl, and I'm fairly certain you bailed out this place when my father ran it into the ground." It was true, but Max had promised Simon's father that he'd never admit it, and he wouldn't. "The rest doesn't matter. Just as I'm guessing it wouldn't have mattered to her."

"It wouldn't have changed anything," he said. "She'd still be gone. She would always have left. Nothing I could say would change that—telling her the truth would only have hastened the inevitable."

There was a long pause, like an eternity.

"It wouldn't have changed anything," Max said, filling it. "She'd still be gone."

Simon watched him for a stretch, and then said, "You look like you've been rolled down the hill and into my pub. How long has she been gone?"

Max shook his head. "I don't know." He'd left her after she'd fallen asleep on the other side of the bed, out of his arms for the first time since the first night. Gone back to his apartments. Woken at dawn without her and returned to the cottage, ready to explain everything, even if it meant losing out on those last few precious days—and nights—at her side. But it had been too late. She'd left.

As he'd always known she would.

"A few hours."

He filled Simon in, telling him the story of their arrangement, designed only to last until Lilah went back to London and returned to her life, filled with celebrities and superstars and leaving no room for Max, who—even if she knew the truth—would never be able to give her what she wanted.

But that wasn't all Max told his friend. He told him about *Lilah*—about her brilliant photographs, and her easy laugh, and the way she'd won him again and again, and made him believe, more and more, that it was possible for him to be Max forever. And her to be Lilah forever. And for them to live in farmhouse idyll forever.

"When she asked me to go with her, I told her I couldn't," he said. He'd watched as disappointment and resignation had clouded her gaze, even as she'd promised him she understood, hating it even as he told himself it was for the best. That it was the best way to keep her from a larger, more devastating disappointment.

To keep from disappointing her.

"Wait. What?" Simon didn't seem to agree. "Why couldn't you go?"

"Because I'm not what she wants. Not really."

"Sorry," said his friend, leaning down on the bar. "I don't follow. Did she or did she not invite you to London to go to this posh party?"

"She did. But she doesn't know that I've been a part of that world, and I can't make her happy in it."

Silence fell, the sound of the rain on the ancient stained glass windows all there was as Simon turned away to fetch the coffee. Only once he'd poured the cup and slid it across the bar to Max, he said, "Would you like to know, Max, what I thought the first time you brought Georgiana to Salterton?" He paused. "What we all thought?"

Max looked to Simon—his oldest friend, who'd always

known about his family and his fortune and never once seemed to care. "I don't suppose I have a choice."

"Ha, no. We all thought you were doomed to unhappiness."

The words were a blow. Max's brow furrowed. "What does that mean?"

"Oh, we threw you a stag and dressed up for church and toasted you heartily and hoped we were wrong, but we could see the truth." Simon backed up to his favorite place for pontificating, against the far wall of the bar, arms crossed over his massive chest. "You and Georgiana whatev-erhernamewas—"

"Chesterton," Max said. "She's Countess of Hyde, now."

"Good for her," Simon retorted. "Point is, the two of you were twenty-three and had the brains to prove it. She was put together as they come—more money than any person needs and reading posh accents at school, or whatever."

"History of Art, actually. And she's not exactly faffing about in Ibiza, Simon. She's head of the British Museum."

"Oh, well, what in hell was she doing with you to begin with, then?"

"That's my point," Max said, lifting the cup. "She shouldn't have been with me. I made her miserable."

"No, you didn't," Simon said. "You made *each other* miserable. She was born for a world with plummy titles and posh friends and her picture in *Tatler* every month, and good for her for realizing that and telling you that she wanted that life and not this one when you were sulking around here, dreaming of a girl who could rate in Wellington boots and didn't mind the stink of your dog."

Atlas sighed in the corner, used to being maligned by Simon, who was still going.

"The point is, you were both wrong. And Lady Hyde is

sorted. Turns out she wasn't doomed to unhappiness after all."

She wasn't. Last he'd heard from her, Georgiana was happy and successful and wildly in love with her husband and children.

It had been a long time since Max had thought about happiness.

No. It wasn't true.

Lilah made him happy.

He looked up, meeting Simon's knowing eyes. "I love her."

"Of course you do," his friend said. "You were half in love with her the other night when you were in here playing darts and flirting up a storm."

It had been the best night of his life. Except for all the others with her.

And still, "I don't want to disappoint her."

"How do you know you will?"

"I know, because she's spent the last eighteen months trying to get back to that world. She's been at the center of it for years—she's met more aristocrats than I have! And when she talks about losing it . . . " Max met his friend's gaze, and was surprised to find sympathy there. "When she talks about losing it, I can tell she'd do anything to get it back. She wants someone who will love it like she does. And I can't be that. I've tried, but I can't."

More than that, he couldn't bear to live through the moment when Lilah realized he wasn't what she thought, wasn't what she wanted, wasn't . . . enough.

"Did you ask her what she wants?"

Max stilled. "No. That wasn't part of the deal. The deal was nine days, until she left."

"Oh, well then, if the deal was nine days, then—"

Simon's words were dry as sand. "Max. Are you saying, this girl asked you—idiot farmer—to stand next to her during one of the most important nights of her life, and you think that wasn't a blatant invitation to a future?"

Max swallowed back frustration at the question. "I've said yes to that invitation before. And I've made a hash of it."

"Well, seems like you're damned if you do and damned if you don't, mate. But one way, you've got the girl." Simon shook his head. "You know what? You're right. You do not deserve that woman. From what I can see, she is brilliant, beautiful, a ringer at darts, and legions too good for you."

It was all true.

"All right," Simon drawled, as though he was speaking to a small child. "How about this? Has it occurred to you that you have enough money to travel the world and take the woman you love to a gala at the British Museum, or a party in New York, or a week in the Maldives because that's what she wants—oh and because she's a fucking superstar you don't deserve—you can do that, and be back here with your sheep and your hay and your dog within hours? Has it occurred to you that what felt like all or nothing at twenty-two might be more nuanced at thirty-five?"

Hope flared.

"Has it occurred to you that you could try again?"

He didn't have to wait here, on the ramparts, terrified she might never return.

They could fight together.

And come home together.

"This isn't the same, bruv," Simon said, not a hint of sarcasm in his tone. "You're not twenty anymore, trying to work out how to become a man and a duke all in one breath.

And she's not twenty, trying to make a go of it in the world and also not disappoint her husband. Lilah Rose is a grown woman who knows what she wants, Max. And—though it flummoxes me more than I can say—it appears she wants you."

"You're an ass," Max said.

"But a brilliant one," Simon retorted. "Why don't you believe her?"

Because no one had ever wanted him for more than that world. From the moment he was born, that had been his value. Access to that world.

Simon seemed to hear the thoughts. He came off the back wall and leaned down, his elbows on the slick mahogany bar. "It might not work out, mate. For any number of reasons, which doesn't make you a special case, by the way. But doesn't Lilah at least deserve the chance to throw you over for the right reason, knowing all the facts? Or to choose to try, eyes wide-open?"

And like that, Max saw it.

He'd been so caught up in thinking about what he could bear and what he couldn't, he'd discounted *Lilah*. Why the hell had he tried to fight this battle alone, when he'd had the strongest, cleverest, most creative and perceptive woman in the world ready and able to help win this war?

Their future was not written.

They could write it. Different. Perfect.

Together.

"And if it doesn't work out," Simon concluded, "you'll come here and drink yourself into a stupor and I'll charge you double for whinging into your pint about how hard it is to be a duke, poor fucking baby."

"I have to tell her who I am."

An idea came, half-formed. Coalescing.

Max felt like one of his marauding ancestors, girding his loins for the battle of his life. "I have to get to her."

"Right then." Simon nodded with satisfaction. "Tell her the dart board is always open for her."

11

The show was a triumph.

The Great Court of the British Museum was awash in warm light, giving the whole space an autumnal feel that Lilah would never have expected from somewhere known for soaring white walls and a roof designed to reveal firmament and nothing else.

And her photos were perfect.

The decorators had followed her careful instructions, hanging the ten enormous prints around the central staircase of the Court, the curves of the room obscuring them until attendees made a full turn of the space. Each one highlighted the work of one of the sustainable farms she'd visited, capturing the people who had devoted themselves to ensuring their land would survive for generations while prioritizing delicate ecosystems.

Seeing them together, Lilah realized why she loved this project—not only because she'd hoped it would return her to the world from which she'd been summarily booted, but because she recognized herself in these people. Passionate. Proud. Purposeful.

And now, she recognized Max in them.

No.

No thinking about Max. He'd made it clear that he had no interest in extending their arrangement beyond the Weston estate. Beyond the nine days they'd promised each other.

Of course, Lilah hadn't given him nine days.

She hadn't been able to, not once she'd realized how much she'd fallen for him in such a short time. Not once she'd realized that he hadn't fallen for her.

We go to war together, he'd promised her that day on the tower.

And yet here she was, in full armor, ready for battle. *Alone.*

Her chest tightened at the thought, enough for her to grab a glass of Prosecco from a passing tray and square her shoulders, willing her heartbeat steady as she entered the room.

She wore a sleek black Paul Smith tux with a cigarette pant that she'd had for years—a nod to sustainability, with the added bonus of it being a comfortable old friend. The deep plunge of the satin lapels revealed a long, narrow wedge of skin. Her hair was wild and loose, a dark, smoky eye finishing the look.

The armor looked good. It had to.

It was her against the world.

Inside, she recognized a handful of people. Some, she'd met and photographed during her travels: a Peruvian economist who had perfected small-batch cacao farming that honored a protected biosphere; a Danish chef who'd made a name bringing foraged food into haute cuisine; the grape growers from California.

Some, she'd encountered before she'd been ruined: an

Academy Award winner with a passion for environmental causes; several CEOs committed to sustainability; a world-renowned Emirati architect specializing in revolutionary green skyscrapers.

The place was a who's who of activist glitterati.

And Lilah, without her Nikon for protection.

Without anyone for protection.

When was the last time she'd walked into a showing of her work without a battalion of people—people who disappeared the moment she'd been blacklisted? People who lacked loyalty and only attached themselves to her when there was something valuable for her to give them.

She didn't need them.

And if she kept her head high, perhaps she'd forget that the only person she wanted wasn't there.

"Lilah!"

She turned to see Aarti Rao coming toward her with a bright smile before pulling her in close for a warm embrace.

"Friend!" Lilah said, unable to contain her relief. "I cannot tell you how happy I am to see your face!" She lowered her voice. "Do people like them?"

Aarti pulled back sharply. "You are kidding. They are *magnificent*. Look at them all, craning their necks to get a better view. No one cares about the rest of this old stuff tonight, darling." Lilah laughed as her friend waved a hand in the direction of the galleries beyond. "I've told everyone who will listen that they absolutely must come and tell you just how perfect they are." She added, softly, "We are very proud to benefit from the return of Lilah Rose."

For the first time that evening, Lilah's smile was authentic. "I'm so happy you're happy with them."

"We're thrilled. And personally, I am planning on using mine as my business card!"

Lilah looked up to the picture of Aarti in the lab on her family's farm in Andhra Pradesh, at the center of nearly a thousand saplings at different stages of growth. The biochemist's arms were crossed, her pride in her achievements clear as day on her lovely, laughing face. "The best day," Lilah recalled. "I want to come back."

"Anytime," her friend said as they began to circle the room. "But I think that after tonight, you're going to be a bit busy."

Lilah's heart pounded at the prediction—everything she'd wanted.

Not everything.

She pushed the thought away. It was not for tonight.

She and Aarti were immediately swallowed by the crowd. The subjects of Lilah's portraits were all in attendance, deep in conversation with stars and businesspeople alike, finding common ground—which was precisely the point of the evening.

Lilah was thrilled.

Aarti's prediction came true as they circled the space; every few feet, they were waylaid by someone coming to meet Lilah—celebrities, fellow artists, the editors-in-chief of two magazines, wealthy attendees looking to discuss commissioned work. She took every introduction in stride, slowly falling back into the habit of having these conversations about her art—about what might come next.

For eighteen months she had planned for this night—knowing it would be important, because it would mark her return to the world from which she'd been exiled. And she could not have asked for a better reception. Suddenly, everything felt possible.

Everything but one thing, which she refused to think on.

One thing that she knew, later that night, back at the hotel, would make her ache.

"You've caught all of us in these beautiful moments," Aarti said as another enormous portrait came into view. Gianna Simeti—an elderly Sicilian woman seated high on an enormous pile of aging cheese wheels on the farm her family had owned since she was a young girl—stared down the lens of Lilah's camera, a lifetime of work in the lines of her face, and a familiar pride in her eyes.

"It's honesty," Lilah said. "You're all in love."

"That's true," Aarti replied, a gleam of something Lilah didn't quite understand in her eyes. "I particularly like the next one."

Lilah followed her gaze to the next photo, the outer edge just in view.

Her brows knit together and a wash of uncertainty flooded her. It wasn't her photo. She shook her head, moving more quickly. "I didn't—"

She stopped short as the image appeared.

It was her shot.

It was the picture of Max she'd taken at the top of the folly at Salterton Abbey, the estate laid out behind him, white pops of sheep and bales of hay and the fields of barley in the distance, turned gold in the late afternoon sun—the same as the gold in his eyes.

She caught her breath, her chest tightening as she drank in the image of him, a whirlwind of emotions coming with the memory of what he'd said immediately after she'd taken it.

You're perfect.

She could hear the words in his low, delicious voice, carrying on the wind, whipping around them on the parapet, just before she'd put her camera away and they'd made love.

It was a gorgeous shot, one that seamlessly integrated with all the others and still felt like it was ripping Lilah's chest open with its honesty. Max had that same look in his eye as all the other farmers.

Pride. Passion. Purpose.

Except he wasn't thinking about the farm in that moment; he was thinking about her.

He was proud of her.

She shook her head again, unable to look away. "How did you get it?"

"The Duke of Weston sent it over himself," Aarti said. "Direct from Salterton Abbey. He said you'd taken a final picture, and he thought we might like it for the event. As he put up the seed money for Common Harvest, we were happy to . . . "

Her friend's words faded away as Lilah craned to see through the throngs of people. "Is he here?"

"The duke? I think so, as a matter of fact. Another late addition," Aarti said. "It's a coup for the organization, as he's notoriously private, so people will be thrilled with the photo."

"No, not the duke," Lilah replied, the words barely there, caught in her throat as she saw him. "*Max.*"

He was beneath his photo, looking nothing like the man above, dressed in a navy peak lapel three-piece suit, the watch chain on the waistcoat thick and modern—reminding her that underneath all that perfect tailoring he knew how to get dirty.

This was a man who was asking to be mussed, and she was absolutely up for the challenge.

Lilah was already moving toward him. "Sorry, Aarti. I see—"

The man I love.

She pushed through the crowd, desperate to get to him.

And then he was there, catching her up in his embrace, and her arms were wrapping around his neck and he was lifting her against him, and she let him, not caring who saw. Caring only that he was here. "You came," she said, like a prayer.

"I should have been here from the start," he rumbled, low and secret. She reveled in the feel of him against her when he set her on her feet, and leaned down to say at her ear, "I want very much to kiss you, but I'm on my best behavior."

She snapped her head around to meet his gaze. "That is a shame, as I would very much like to be kissed by someone not on his best behavior."

"Mmm," he growled, the breath of air at her neck sending a shiver of pleasure only enhanced by the large, warm hand sliding to the small of her back. "You really ought to provide a warning when turning out looking like you do, Lilah Rose." He slid the tip of one finger just beneath the edge of her lapel, setting the skin beneath aflame as he teased, "I am glad I am here, as this kirtle does not look as though it has room for a blade."

She grinned. "No battle necessary."

He shook his head. "Instant victory."

"It feels like victory now that you're here."

He lifted his hand to her cheek, rubbing his thumb across her skin, like he'd missed her. She closed her eyes at the touch. She had missed him. When she opened her eyes, he was there, watching her, and he said, low and purposeful, "I'll always be here, Lilah. As long as you'll have me."

And she believed him.

"Do you forgive me for sending the photo? I know it wasn't part of the set, but Salterton is sustainable, and I thought—"

"Shh." She looked up at it—one of the best she'd ever taken. "As grand gestures go, it's perfect."

"You're perfect," he said, an echo of the words he'd spoken the moment after she'd taken that picture.

"I'm so happy you came," she said, the success of the evening more rewarding now that he was there.

He pressed a kiss to the corner of her mouth, then another high on one cheek. "Your photographs—they're incredible. Show them to me?"

Speeches had begun, so they toured the massive prints in relative privacy, hand-in-hand, Lilah quietly telling him about each of the farms she'd visited. He listened like the perfect date, riveted to the images and her stories.

Lilah, too, was riveted—to the way he looked at her work, admiration and pleasure in his gaze. Pride. In her.

And there, in that room that had returned her to the world, Lilah realized that the time with Max had done something more. It had returned her to herself.

When they were once again at his portrait, Max took his cue, and Lilah laughed as he tugged her across the room, barely avoiding a collision with a pretty blond server.

Tucking into a little alcove off the Court, he wrapped his arms around Lilah's waist, stealing kisses down the column of her neck. She sighed in his embrace, wrapping her own arms around his neck. "I missed you."

"Not like I've missed you," he whispered at the place where her pulse pounded. "I can't sleep. Mabel won't even look at me. Simon says I'm naff at women."

She giggled. "You're not naff at me."

"I was, though. I thought I would disappoint you."

"How could you possibly think that?"

He hesitated, and for a split second—barely an instant—something flashed in his eyes. Lilah saw it, wishing she had her camera. Wishing she could study it. Identify it. But in that moment, she couldn't name it beyond a keen sense that Max had more to say.

"Max?"

He shook his head. "This night, here, it's yours. Everything else will keep." He looked past her to the enormous room, a thousand people in revelry. "They love you."

"No. They love what I do. They love what I can make people feel. What I can make them see. But they don't love me. They don't know me. I'm just the girl behind the camera."

"I know you," he said. Her heart began to pound as he tilted her chin up, meeting her gaze. "I love you."

She closed her eyes, her breath tight in her chest. "Max—"

"Let me finish. Whatever tonight brings. Wherever it takes you. I want to be by your side." He paused and then he said, "Not that you need me."

Tears sprang at the words. *I do need you.*

He was still talking. "I know it's fast. I know we've only known each other for a heartbeat. But I want to be with you. I want to love you. And I'll wait for you as long as I need to."

"Max," she said. "I think you might, in fact, be naff at women."

His brow furrowed. "What does that mean?"

"It means I love you too, you numpty."

He pulled her tight to him with a low, delicious laugh. "It's not quite the delivery I was hoping for, but I probably deserve it."

She grinned. "Definitely. You *definitely* deserve it."

He slipped a finger into the opening of her jacket again. Slightly farther this time. Enough to send shivers of pleasure through her. "I am very open to doing penance," he said, low and dark.

"I can think of a thing or two," she replied, desperate for him.

"Quickly," he growled, pulling her deeper into the alcove, out of the view of anyone who wasn't expressly looking, and tipped her chin up to press a lingering kiss on her neck. "I promise I won't muss you, belle of the ball."

She threaded her fingers into his hair. "I can't make the same promises."

His laugh was swallowed by a low curse when he opened the single button of her jacket and spread the fabric, revealing her bare breasts. "So beautiful. You are going to kill me, Lilah Rose."

He dipped his head and took one straining tip into his mouth, suckling in long, deep pulls that had her writhing against him. "Max."

"Mmm. I'll stop," he said. "But it wouldn't be fair if—"

"No," she gasped, the words hushed and fervent. "It really wouldn't."

She gave a tiny cry when he took her other nipple into his mouth, his thigh coming between hers, pressing against the place she desperately wanted him. And for a moment Lilah writhed there, rocking herself against him, slow and firm, just enough to set herself on fire. Mistake.

She cursed her frustration when Max pulled away, buttoning her jacket as he rained kisses on her cheeks and temple, whispering a wicked curse there before saying, "That is going to ruin me for the rest of the evening."

"Let's go," she said. "My hotel is a five-minute walk."

He shook his head. "No. This is your night."

"Exactly," she said, no longer caring about anything but this moment, this man. The photos would be here tomorrow. Tomorrow, she'd hit the pavement. Find a new agent. Start fresh and aim for everything she wanted.

And she'd get it.

But tonight, she wanted Max. "This is my night, and I want to go." She stroked over the front of his trousers, finding his cock firm within. "I'm happy to leave them wanting."

"Poor bastards, I know how they'll feel," he quipped, letting her pull him out of the alcove, back toward the entrance to the hall.

They'd gotten no more than a few feet when a man stepped into their path.

"Hello, Miss Rose."

At the words, delivered in a nasal, American drawl, Lilah skidded to a stop. Her spine straightened as her skin crawled, but she was already turning—there was no other option on the table. And there, tall and reed-thin in an ill-fitting suit that did nothing for his pasty skin, was Jeffrey Greenwood, multi-millionaire, media mogul, creep, and the man who had destroyed her career.

12

Lilah hesitated, not knowing how to respond. Wanting to ignore him. Wanting to tell him off. Wanting to run.

But she wasn't alone anymore.

Max was immediately by her side. "What's wrong?"

"My studio is making a movie with Marcus Anderssen," Greenwood said, pointing to the handsome young actor in the distance, known for his passion for environmental causes. The producer's ice-blue eyes were calculating as he smiled without warmth. "Had I known you were taking these photos, I would have made a much larger contribution." He chuckled, the sound humorless, and pulled a glass of wine off a passing tray. "Next time, I suppose."

The threat was clear as day. Not really a threat. More of a promise. He had enough money to ruin Lilah again and again. For kicks.

Frustration flared, then unbridled anger when Greenwood turned to Max. Easy Max. Wonderful Max, who she didn't want anywhere near this. He extended his hand and said, "Jeffrey Greenwood. Miss Rose took some pictures of me once."

Max couldn't have looked calmer as he clasped the offered hand. "I hear they never made the light of day."

Greenwood's gaze narrowed with understanding, and he tried to pull away. Max wasn't having it.

"Lilah," Max said. "Look at me."

She did, and he read it all. Every truth. Every desire.

He threw the punch before she could stop him.

"Max! Shit!" Lilah said as Greenwood went down with a screech, blood exploding from his nose. "You can't punch him!"

"Too fucking late," he said, shaking out his fist. "We go to war together, remember?"

He was magnificent.

"Oh my God," she said, delight and surprise and horror flooding her before concern for Max won out. She grabbed his hand and checked his knuckles. "You've hurt yourself!"

"Worth it."

She couldn't help the little hysterical laugh that came at the words. "Oh my God," she repeated. A bright light registered in her peripheral vision. An iPhone. "Too bad you didn't start that Instagram account," she said. "You're about to go viral."

"I don't care," he said, staring down at the bastard who'd ruined her career. "I hope they got every second of it."

And then, from below, "You broke my nose, you asshole! I don't know who you are, but I'm going to fucking sue you into the ground. And your *girlfriend* will go back to not being able to get a job anywhere. The local shelter won't let her take pictures of *strays*. You don't know who you fucked with."

Max stiffened beneath her touch, turning to steel.

Panic flared. "Max. Don't. It's not worth it."

"No," he replied, his voice cold and unyielding as he lowered himself to a crouch, sending Greenwood scrambling back. Not fast enough. Max's hand shot out and he grabbed a fistful of the disgusting man's jacket, holding him still. "You don't know who *you've* fucked with. How dare you think yourself worthy of her. How dare you think yourself worthy of looking at her. At her art." The words were no longer cold; they dripped with disdain. "How dare you think yourself worthy of speaking her name." He tightened his fist and pulled the other man closer. "If you come for her again, I will destroy you. Don't doubt it."

God, she loved this man. She loved how willing he was to protect her. How proud he was of her. How proud he was to stand with her.

"Max." He released Greenwood the second she spoke his name, rising without difficulty. He took a handkerchief from his pocket and wiped his hands, and in that moment, in that beautiful pause, he looked nothing like her Max. He looked like pure, leashed power. Expensive and undeniable.

Don't blink.

Several well-dressed security guards arrived as Greenwood scrambled to his feet. One reached to help him. "Get your hands off me. Worry about him." He waved a hand in Max's direction. "That . . . *animal* . . . assaulted me."

Time to go. Lilah didn't want to have to bail Max out of jail tonight. Was it even called jail here? "That's our cue."

Max was in no hurry. He returned his handkerchief to his pocket and straightened the cuff of his jacket. "We're not going anywhere."

What the hell was wrong with him? "We're not?"

A crowd had collected, phones out, and Lilah could already hear the whispers. Her name. Greenwood's.

Who's the other one?

He's mine, Lilah thought.

"Sir," one of the security guards said to him, "I'm sorry, but you'll have to come with me."

"No, I don't think I will."

"Max," she said quietly. "What are you doing?"

She could see the murderous look in his eyes. "What I am doing and what I want to do are very different things."

Before she could reply, a shocked voice called out, "Weston! What on earth is going on here?" Lilah recognized the tall, stunningly beautiful Black woman in a claret vintage silk Cushnie sheath moving toward them at a clip—Dr. Georgiana Chesterton, the director of the museum.

It wasn't exactly the way Lilah had envisioned meeting one of the greatest minds in art, but life came at you fast.

Dr. Chesterton's attention was moving back and forth between Max and the security guard who had frozen in the act of forcibly removing him. "I don't know what you think you are doing, but this is the Duke of Weston. Unhand him, please."

What?

Lilah turned in shocked surprise to Max, expecting him to wink at her with one of those slow, easy smiles, a laughing denial.

But there was no smile.

In the hesitation, she saw the truth. "Max?"

More hesitation. More truth.

Only this time, Lilah didn't want to see it.

"Once more, this is the Duke of Weston," Dr. Chesterton said firmly, as though no one had heard her at first. "Weston of the *Weston Galleries*," she underscored, pointing to the bronzed words installed above a nearby doorway.

The security guard immediately released Max, who rolled his shoulders back. "Cheers, mate."

The woman gave Max a look that indicated more than passing acquaintance. "I confess I, too, am surprised, as in my experience, causing scenes is not the duke's favorite pastime."

He shrugged. "Times change."

Dr. Chesterton sighed. "Do they have to change in my museum?" She waved to a security guard standing nearby, who looked absolutely flummoxed as to how to handle whatever was going on.

Lilah understood exactly how he felt.

"Jonathan, do you mind escorting Mr. Greenwood to my offices?"

"I don't need escorting anywhere, I need the police. I'm calling my lawyer." He pointed at Max and repeated his threat—one that continued to have no impact. "I'm going to sue you into the ground."

Dr. Chesterton smiled, the portrait of expensive composure. "I simply thought you'd like an opportunity to collect yourself. Perhaps do a bit of research about who, exactly, the Duke of Weston is. Of course, you are welcome to suit yourself." Finished, she turned her back on Greenwood, as though he was no one.

Lilah's brows shot up in admiration. This woman was incredible.

"You'd better have had a good reason for causing a scene, Rupert."

Rupert. Rupert Maximillian Arden.

"I swear I do," he replied, still looking at Lilah.

Dr. Chesterton followed his attention. "I see," she said, a bright smile blooming, as though everything about the evening was perfectly ordinary. "Ms. Rose, if I may? I am a great admirer of your work. I particularly like tonight's photograph from Salterton Abbey."

Lilah must have thanked her, but she couldn't remember doing it. The next thing she knew, she was watching Dr. Georgiana Chesterton disappear into the crowd, all elegance and grace.

Georgiana. Rupert. "You were married to her."

"Yes." No hesitation.

"And you are . . . Weston."

The pieces fell into place. The disdain for paparazzi. The men in the pub. The apartments in the estate house. Lottie. All his strange little hesitations whenever she invoked the duke's name. Whenever she talked about the estate.

Max was the fucking duke.

The crowd around them was already dispersing, headed for drinks and dancing now that Greenwood had skulked off and there was nothing left to watch.

Apparently, Lilah's breaking heart was not worthy of a vid.

"I was going to tell you," he said, softly.

She met his eyes. "When?"

"A thousand times."

"Well gosh, Max, I can see how you didn't get around to it. What with all those days we had together." He winced at the words. "I don't understand. Was it a joke?"

"No. Christ. *No.*" His fingers grazed her arm, leaving fire in their wake, her body instantly remembering that he'd just stretched it tight like a string and it would like its promised orgasm, thank you very much.

Her body had not received the message that he was a lying bastard.

Nope. Not a bastard. A *duke.*

She pulled away from his touch. "Don't." She was hot with embarrassment. "You lied to me."

"It wasn't a lie . . . "

"I thought you were a *farmer*."

"I am a farmer."

"That's your play? *I'm a farmer*? I asked you if you owned a *suit*!" God, it was mortifying. Of course he owned a suit. He'd turned up in *Gucci,* for fuck's sake, and not off the rack —bespoke as hell and looking like he'd stepped off the pages of *Vogue*.

She'd invited him to this gala, filled with her work, where she'd laid herself bare for him, desperate for his approval, thinking he'd be *impressed* with her. And he was a *duke*. She laughed. "And then, when I saw you here, I thought you were—"

She stopped, not wanting to reveal more of herself to him.

He pounced. "What? What did you think I was?"

I thought you were mine. I thought you were my partner. Us against the world.

I thought you were my future.

And it turned out, he was a duke. The most glamorous guest at this party filled with glamorous people. And Lilah? She was back to where she always was.

Alone.

I thought you were home.

"Lilah," he said softly, stepping closer. "Please. I wanted to tell you."

Don't touch me. Don't make it harder.

"And how did that end? You reveal you're secretly a duke and I throw myself into your arms and we live happily ever after . . . cosplaying in your collection of medieval suits of armor?"

He blinked. "Is that what you think we would do?"

"I don't know what *your kind* do."

"Lilah," he started, cautiously, but she could tell he was holding back a smile, and she considered giving the British Museum a second punch in the face that evening. "I don't own suits of armor, but I will get some if that's what you'd like."

"Don't," she said. "Don't make this a joke. You lied to me." She turned on her heel and made for the door. Max was at her elbow instantly. "I should have known. Look at you. Of course you're a duke. With your perfect face and your perfect voice and your . . . *watch*."

"What? What about my watch?"

She cut him a look. "I thought it was a gift! But it wasn't, was it? It's just a normal twenty-thousand-dollar watch that you wear on regular days in a sheep pasture *because you're a duke*." She stopped at the coat check, empty now that everyone was inside, enjoying themselves. She spun to face him. "Is this some kind of bullshit game you play with all the girls who wander onto your estate? See if you can get them to bang the hot farmer?"

"What? No!"

She turned her back on him, digging a small white rectangle from her pocket, and passed it to the young woman behind the counter who stared at them, wide-eyed. "Thank you," she said, but what she meant was *Please, God, hurry*.

"Lilah—listen to me."

"No. You listen to me," she said, anger coming hot and furious. "I've spent the last eighteen months of my life trying to put myself back together, trying to work up the courage to trust this world again—this world that turned its back on me. And you—" Tears came, hot and unbidden, and she willed them back. "No. Not you. *Max* made me believe that it was possible. That I could trust again. That I could believe in the value of my work and in my own value.. And that I could open myself up again, and triumph, and maybe . . . just maybe . . . also get the guy."

"You got the guy," he said. "I'm here."

"I didn't even know your *name*."

"Who cares about my fucking name?"

Weston.

Rupert Maximillian Arden. Fourteenth Duke of Weston, Earl Salterton.

That strange, foreign, mystery of a name—the name used with reverence by the staff in the estate house, the one they'd casually tossed around while they'd joked with the boys in the pub, while they'd walked to the folly tower on the edge of the estate, where she'd realized how fast she was falling in love.

And all the while *he'd* been the duke.

He wasn't *Max*.

God, she hadn't even asked him his last name.

Her face went hot with refreshed embarrassment. The laughter in the pub—the way they'd all guffawed and winked along with her when she'd talked about how she didn't trust rich and powerful men. And all that time, the joke hadn't been on the duke in the castle on the hill.

It had been on her.

Because Max *was* the duke in the castle on the hill.

"Obviously you care about your name a whole lot, Max, or you would have introduced yourself."

He rocked back on his heels, and she turned back to the woman in the coat check. "Thank you," she said, collecting her coat, clutching it to her chest. Armor.

She met his eyes then, those beautiful, whiskey-colored

eyes she'd imagined looking into for the rest of her life. Now, somehow, in the face of another man.

Max was gone.

And of all the things she'd lost, this one might be the one that broke her.

Her chest tightened, tears threatening.

She would not cry. Not tonight. Not here.

Which meant she had to leave.

"Goodbye, Max."

13

He'd been so close to telling her.

He'd had a plan. Back to her hotel room, and there he'd confess all of it. He'd tell her he was a duke, and why he'd kept it from her.

He'd tell her that he loved her, and that he didn't want a life in half measures. That he wanted all of it. That he wanted her in his world—no more farmhouse idyll, but real life. That he wanted to be in her world, however it came. Real life. Not just the gala. London, New York, Los Angeles—whatever she wanted.

He'd tell her the truth. That he couldn't imagine the future without her, wherever and whenever and however it came.

And then he would make love to her as Weston and as Max, and give her everything he had.

He'd been so close.

But Max should have known better. Because nothing with Lilah had ever gone to plan, since he found her on the ground, taking pictures of his sheep.

Christ, he'd fucked up. Again.

He watched her leave, pushing through a crowd of people that had congregated by the entrance to the museum, wanting more than anything to follow her. Maybe if he followed her, she would—

"I almost couldn't believe it was you, you know."

Max turned toward the words, finding his ex-wife watching him in that way she always had, calm and understanding, like she was perpetually one step ahead of him. And maybe she always had been.

She smiled, warm and full of fondness. "Surely not, I said to myself. Rupert? In London? By *choice*?"

"I come to London," he grumbled.

"Under duress," she said with a little laugh. "But you're not here under duress, are you?"

"No." He'd go anywhere if it meant being with Lilah.

"You're here for Lilah Rose." Her gaze tracked over his shoulder, to the place behind him where Lilah had disappeared. "Have you taken up an interest in photography?"

"Hers," he said.

Georgiana nodded. "I can understand why. She's set the standard for a generation of portrait photographers."

A pause as they stood in silence, as they had a thousand times before, at school, beyond. Finally, Max exhaled. "I really bollocksed it, Georgie."

"Why, because you thrashed Jeffrey Greenwood? I've no idea what he did, but anyone with sense can see he deserved it."

"And more," Max replied. "But it has nothing to do with Greenwood. It has to do with the fact that she didn't know I was Weston."

"What?" When he didn't look at her, Georgiana said in her firmest voice, "Rupert."

He did look then. "You needn't talk to me as though I'm a child. How are your children by the way? And Hyde?"

"They are all fine, thank you, but I've no interest whatsoever in discussing them right now," she said, the words coming in a perfect aristocratic clip. "How long have you known her?"

"Two weeks."

"And you didn't tell her."

"No."

"That you're the duke."

"Christ, Georgiana. No. I didn't."

"Right," she said, turning and pointing back at the Great Court, to the massive pictures. "Look."

Max did as he was told. There he was, on the folly tower at Salterton, acres of land spread out behind him. Hay he'd baled. Sheep he'd lambed.

All of it captured by Lilah. And now, none of it important without her.

"In all the years we were together—" Georgiana said, "You never looked at me like that."

No one cares who is behind the camera.

He cared. Christ, he'd never cared so much.

"You're in love with her."

He looked to his ex-wife. "Yes."

She sighed, the sound full of pity. "Roo."

"I didn't want her to . . . " He trailed off.

Georgiana finished for him. "You didn't want her to love you for the title, and you not be able to deliver."

He didn't reply. He didn't have to.

"Congratulations. She doesn't love you for your title." Her gaze softened. "And I know you never believed it . . . but I didn't love you for it either. It wasn't the title that ended us. It wasn't the sheep, and it wasn't parties in London."

Max looked to the woman he'd married an age ago, believing that they could love each other enough to give up the lives they'd always wanted. "We never wanted the same things."

She smiled, sad and kind. "No, Roo. We were young and silly and we didn't know what we wanted."

He knew what he wanted now though.

"I want her," he said, to himself as much as to Georgiana.

"I'm very happy to hear it. It's rather wonderful when it all falls into place." She smiled the smile of a woman who'd learned that lesson well. "And does she want you?"

"She wants Max."

"Lucky thing, that," Georgiana said. "As you've always been more Max than Weston."

He looked to her. "I love her."

She smiled. "Then I suggest you go tell her. And please thank her for her gorgeous photographs. From me. And when it's sorted, come round to dinner sometime."

He was already gone, headed to the door at a clip no gentleman would ever use in public, but Max had already broken several of the cardinal rules of gentlemen that evening, so there was no reason for him to stop now.

He pushed through the crowd at the door, a plan already forming. She was at a hotel five minutes' walk from the museum. He'd go to every one of them he could find in that radius, all night long until he found her.

He didn't have to go far.

Max burst onto the red carpet, ready to sprint to the street, to discover that something had happened outside—a commotion of some sort, if the police and photographers were any indication. Whatever had occurred was over now, but the gates leading onto Great Russell Street were closed, penning in anyone who wanted to leave.

Which worked out very well for Max, because there, standing at the center of the red carpet, somehow all alone in a pool of light, waiting for the gates to open, was Lilah.

Relief thrummed through him on a wave of adrenaline as he bounded down the steps, calling her name, loving the way she turned, instantly, as though she couldn't help herself.

Good. He couldn't help himself either.

He wanted to turn whenever she called his name. Always.

He came to a stop in front of her, hating the way she'd crossed her arms over her chest, closing herself to him. Protecting herself from him. God. He'd done this to her—all the times he'd wanted to protect her, and now he'd hurt her.

"I love you," he began. "Whatever else there is, whatever else you believe, whatever else you think, know that. I love you. This was not a joke. And it was not a game. And it was not a lie. I might have ruined it, but that is the truth. And that will be true forever. I love you."

She met his eyes then, and he sucked in a breath.

It wasn't enough.

"How can I believe that? I unraveled for you. I told you everything. I held nothing back. I gave you . . . " She paused, and the ache in Max's chest became pain. "I gave you every bit of me. All of it. And you lied to me. From the start."

"I never lied to you," Max insisted, fear and panic thrumming through him as she cut him a look of utter disbelief. She was slipping through his grasp. "I didn't. Christ, Lilah . . . I told you more of my truth than I've ever told anyone. You . . . *you* unraveled *me*. The moment you looked up at me in that pasture . . . I was blown open. I didn't tell you my name. But I told you so much more."

The disbelief was gone now, replaced by something else.

Something like doubt. He could work with doubt. It wasn't ideal, but he could work with it. He stepped closer to her. She didn't back away. He could work with that too. "If you give me the chance, I'll tell you everything. Whatever you want to know. Every dark secret, every embarrassing moment, every emotion." He paused. "I'll start right now. I'm fucking terrified, love. I'm terrified I've lost you."

"God, Max. You make it sound so easy."

"It's always felt easy with us."

Her lips curved in a little smile, and a sliver of hope flared.

"Lilah, love." He was desperate to touch her. He took a lock of her gorgeous hair in hand, the only touch he'd let himself have. "Let me prove it."

There was a low rumble of murmurs somewhere off to the left, but Max didn't look. He was too busy looking at her.

Lilah did look.

"Max," she said, quietly, shooting a nervous glance at the lines of cameras set up on either side of the red carpet. "We're in full view of every tabloid photographer in London. This isn't exactly the place for—"

"I don't care," he said. "I've spent the last decade avoiding them. But I don't care about any of that now. Let them take their pictures. None of it matters. Not if I don't have you. And I can't have you if I don't tell you the truth, which I should have told you from the start."

She nodded. "Okay."

"My father died when I was sixteen."

Her gaze softened. "I'm sorry."

Of course she would say that. Of course that would be her first thought. God, if he lost this woman, he didn't know what he'd do.

"Before that, I was a lot of things. I was born Earl Salterton. I was Arden to schoolmates and Rupert to my family. Lottie called me Roo. Georgiana as well."

Her lips curved in a ghost of a smile. There and gone, so fast that he almost missed it. But he didn't miss it. He loved it. "I know. *Awful.* I hated it, truly. But you know what I hated most? I hated that when my father died, *every* friend I had . . . *every one* . . . immediately started calling me Weston. Without hesitation. One moment I was Rupert or Arden, and then the phone rang at Eton and the news traveled from one room to the next, and instantly I was Weston. My father, not even cold in his grave. As though they'd all been calling me that in their head for years, anyway, just biding their time until they could tell the world that they were friends with a duke."

Her brows knit together as he continued.

"And it happened like *that.*" He snapped his fingers. "Without anyone even thinking to check on me, or to tell me they were sorry that my father had died, I was just someone else. The door closed on the past. Opened on some new future. Time to learn how to live in it." He stilled, thinking on it. Hating that he still remembered the ache of it. Dwelled on it. He scoffed. "But what a whinge, right? I was a duke, and it came with money and power and privilege beyond reason, and everything I could ever ask for. And here I am, complaining that people noticed."

"You were sixteen. And even if you weren't . . . it was your life." She reached up to touch him, her fingers sliding over his cheek, and he closed his eyes, the pleasure of her touch nearly unbearable.

She wouldn't touch him if he'd lost her, would she?

"One minute you were there, and the next you were gone." At her words, his gaze flew to hers, finding tears in her beautiful eyes.

Christ, he loved her.

"Max," she whispered, searching his face.

"No." He took her hand in his and kissed her fingertips. "Let me finish. I was born into this world. Power and privilege and money, with duty to the title absolutely drilled into me from birth. And I was terrible at this part of it." He waved a hand at the museum, large and looming behind her. "I hated being here, in London. I hated parties and people and . . . "

"Paparazzi?"

He nodded. "Them too. And I thought that if you wanted all this, I was doomed to disappoint you." He hesitated, searching for the explanation. "So I stayed Max, telling myself I'd let you go at the end of our time together. Telling myself I'd be able to watch you return to your world and not wildly, desperately, want to be a part of it so I could be near you. Telling myself I could be in love with you and still let you go."

"You should have asked me," she said, her brow furrowing.

"I know."

"You almost broke both our hearts."

"I know. I'm sorry."

She nodded, her eyes searching his. Laying him bare. "No more of that."

"None. I swear it."

She smiled then, small and sweet. "Let's go back to you wanting to be near me."

The tightness in his chest loosened. "Every minute of every day. Wherever you want to be."

"That doesn't sound like it could possibly disappoint me," she said, a gleam of something like happiness in her beautiful eyes. "But it's not all or nothing. This world . . . it's not my world anymore. It's not all I have. It's my work, and I love it, and I don't want to leave it. But there are other things I love. Other things I don't want to leave. Like you. Like Salterton."

Yes.

"Then don't," he said. "You never have to."

She looked him up and down, and he took the way her appraising gaze turned hungry as an extremely positive sign. "Though, truthfully, any time you want to put on this suit and tag along for work, I'm not going to say no."

He laughed. "I think I can manage that."

She stepped toward him, close enough that he could feel her heat. "A duke, huh?"

"I should have told you," he repeated. "I'm sorry. But the idea that a woman like you—brilliant, talented, sexy as hell—would love me . . . *Max* . . . me . . . without any of the rest of it . . . I was terrified of ruining it." He exhaled and looked up at the sky, then looked back at her. "It was like a gift. In all my life before you, I've never been enough. Just me, on my own."

"Max," she said, lifting her hand, pushing a lock of hair from his brow. "I love *you*. I love you, and the men in the Fox and Falcon, and your enormous dog, and your terrifying sheep, and your cottage, and your *Aga* . . . " He laughed again. "And if they come with a title, well, I suppose I'm going to have to try falling in love with the duke too."

"I'm afraid he's the only way you get the bespoke suits."

She laughed. "Well then, I will persevere. I'll get used to the whole world calling you Weston, as long as I can save Weston for special occasions, and call you Max all the rest of the time."

He set his forehead to hers. "Yes, please. Now kiss me."

"If we do that, the Duke of Weston will return with a bang, whether you like it or not."

"If it means you kiss me, I promise I'll like it."

Dozens of camera flashes fired as he lowered his lips to hers, a slow, sinful temptation.

"Max?" she whispered, just before he kissed her.

"Mmm?"

"Don't blink."

EPILOGUE

Five months later, Lilah opened the door to the cottage, weary from her overnight flight from Los Angeles and the drive from Heathrow. Dropping her bag in the foyer, she called out for Max.

No answer.

She took off her shoes and made her way to the kitchen, stopping to wash her hands and face. She reveled in the quiet peace of the creaky old house—so different from where she'd been two nights earlier, in the delicious mayhem of the Oscars.

Aarti had been right—after the Common Harvest gala, Lilah was welcomed back into the world she'd once thought was everything. Greenwood had tried to bury her again—as powerful men so often did—but this time, Lilah stood alongside a dozen other women he'd threatened and harmed, and they'd told their stories together.

It had been Greenwood who was buried, and she'd be lying if she said her time in Los Angeles hadn't been sweeter for that triumph.

Lilah had spent the day of the awards shadowing a young nominee during her first red carpet prep, and the evening taking a collection of group portraits at the *Bonfire* After Party.

Years earlier, she might have spent the rest of the week in a haze of lunches and drinks and dinners and networking —or she would have taken one of the half dozen interviews she'd been offered, in the hopes she might share salacious details of the downfall of Greenwood. But Lilah had something far more tempting waiting for her at home.

Max.

The kitchen was empty, late afternoon sunlight pouring through the windows overlooking the wide expanse of green spring pastures beyond. She paused for a heartbeat to take in the view—one of the many reasons they'd decided to live here, in the cottage, and save the estate house for special occasions.

There, on the scarred kitchen table, was a note in Max's bold scrawl.

Checking on Mabel.
I love you.

She smiled. Even as he'd dashed off the note, he'd added his love. As though she might not know. As though he hadn't told her he loved her several times a day since the night he'd told her the first time.

Slipping the paper into her back pocket, she went to the rear door of the cottage, pulled on her wellies, and set off to find him, the thought of him chasing away jet lag and exhaustion. She crested the hill a few hundred yards from the cottage, looking down on the field below, dotted with sheep, Atlas in the distance.

And there, in the center of all of it, was Max. Holding a lamb.

Lilah's chest tightened at the image—her big, broad farmer cradling the little creature—and her stomach flipped with pleasure, hormones standing up and taking notice. It was ridiculous how easy it was to love him.

He looked up as she made her way toward him, his eyes lighting with pleasure before he crouched to set the little creature on the ground and came for her, long strides eating up the green earth. Lilah laughed, distracted by the lamb stumbling and swaying toward Mabel—who immediately provided shelter.

And then Max was there, catching her to him, lifting her high in his arms and kissing her, deep and thorough and desperate enough that anyone watching would think they'd been apart for months instead of a few short days. Lilah met the kiss, just as thorough, just as desperate.

Wildly in love with this man, farmer, duke, marauder, *hers*.

When they finally came up for air, he set her back on her feet, Atlas dancing around them for a hello. "I love it when you come home."

She smiled and said, "I love coming home." She leaned over to give the dog some attention, then peeked past Max to see the lamb. "And you, just hanging out in a field, holding a new lamb. Could you be more picturesque?"

"Mabel and I have always liked making the place nice for you."

She laughed, tucking herself into the crook of his arm as they made their way over to the ewe. "Well done, Mabes," she said, and Mabel seemed to preen under the compliment. Lilah crouched and called to the lamb, who came immediately to her, curious and sweet.

Lilah went to her knees, the two-day-old lamb coming to stand on her thighs, accepting her touch instantly. She lifted it into her arms, cuddling it close. "What a love."

"He likes your touch. I can relate."

She flashed him a grin over the lamb's fluffy white head. "Passionate-shepherd-to-his-lady-love flirting is the best kind of flirting." Lifting the little creature into the air, she studied its sweet face and said "I think we should name you Marlowe."

The lamb gave a tiny, high-pitched bleat and squirmed to be free, and Lilah released it to the field and its mother with a laugh. Brushing mud and grass from her thighs, she stood, Max reaching down to help her up.

Her laugh caught in her throat as she met his gaze, hot and delicious on her.

"Marry me."

She stilled, surprise and a deep, delicious pleasure coursing through her. Had she heard it correctly? "What did you say?"

He cradled her face in his warm, rough hands, tilting her up to him, until she was lost in his whiskey eyes. "I've resisted asking you that for months. I've wanted to ask you every day since the day you left for London. I wanted to ask you at the British Museum under your gorgeous photographs, and in the kitchen at the cottage, and in the gift shop of the main house that day when you made me go in and introduce myself to the guests."

She laughed, delighted by him and the memory. He'd hated it. And then he'd loved it. "Really?"

"Yes, really. I wanted to ask you when we were in the States for Thanksgiving with your friends. And when we spent Christmas here at the Abbey with Lottie and Jez and Simon. And every night we've spent at the pub, and again, as we've walked home under the stars."

She wrapped her arms around his waist, wanting to scream her answer and also to savor this moment—one she wanted to remember for the rest of her days. "Why haven't you?"

"Because I wanted to give you time," he said, softly. "To settle back into your brilliant life. To decide that this is enough." He paused. "That I am enough."

She kissed him then, soft and sweet, breaking it to whisper at his lips, "This is perfect. *You* are perfect."

He pulled her tight to him. "Is that what you've decided?"

"I've known it from the start." She paused, then added, "Ask me again."

He smiled, that handsome, crooked smile that stole her breath. "Lilah Rose, will you marry me?"

Max.

"Yes."

He kissed her again, until they were both gasping for breath, and he lifted her high off the ground, her arms wrapping around his neck. She sighed in his arms and said, "Ask me again."

He pressed a kiss to her cheek. "Will you marry me?"

The Duke.

"Yes," she said, turning to catch his lips once more, kissing him until he rumbled his pleasure and lifted her high in his arms, until her legs were wrapped around his waist and he was already crossing the pasture.

"Time to go home," he said. "Now that you've said it twice, I intend to spend the night making you scream it."

The Marauder.

She laughed, full of hope and love and the future . . . and let him lead the way home.

ALSO BY SARAH MACLEAN

Hell's Belles

Knockout

Heartbreaker

Bombshell

The Bareknuckle Bastards

Wicked and the Wallflower

Brazen and the Beast

Daring and the Duke

Scandal & Scoundrel

The Rogue Not Taken

A Scot in the Dark

The Day of the Duchess

The Rules of Scoundrels

A Rogue by Any Other Name

One Good Earl Deserves a Lover

No Good Duke Goes Unpunished

Never Judge a Lady By Her Cover

Love By Numbers

Nine Rules to Break When Romancing a Rake

Ten Ways to be Adored When Landing a Lord

Eleven Scandals to Start to Win a Duke's Heart

Short Stories

The Bladesmith Queen

(available with newsletter sign-up

at sarahmaclean.net)

Young Adult

The Season

Anthologies

How The Dukes Stole Christmas

Generation Wonder

ABOUT THE AUTHOR

New York Times, Washington Post & *USA Today* bestseller Sarah MacLean is the author of historical romance novels. Translated into more than twenty-five languages, the books that make up “The MacLeaniverse” are beloved by readers worldwide.

In addition to her novels, Sarah is a leading advocate for the romance genre, speaking widely on its place as a feminist text and a cultural bellwether. A columnist for the *New York Times*, the *Washington Post* and *Bustle*, she is the co-host of the weekly romance podcast, *Fated Mates*. Her work in support of romance and those who read it earned her a place on Jezebel.com's Sheroes list and led *Entertainment Weekly* to call her "the elegantly fuming, utterly intoxicating queen of historical romance."

Sarah is a graduate of Smith College & Harvard University. She lives in New York City. Find her at sarahmaclean.net or fatedmates.net.

Made in the USA
Las Vegas, NV
08 December 2024

13174171R00100